ONE HUNDRED YEARS WITHOUT LOVE
SANDER M. LEVINE

One Hundred Years Without Love is a work of fiction.
All incidents and dialogue, and all characters with the exception
of historical figures, come from the author's imagination.
In all other respects, any resemblance to any actual persons,
living or dead, businesses, companies, events, or locales
is entirely coincidental.

Copyright @ 2024 by Sander M. Levine
Interior build by Will Robertson

All rights reserved. Except for use in any review,
no part of this book may be reproduced by any means
without written permission from the publisher.

ONE HUNDRED YEARS WITHOUT LOVE
SANDER M. LEVINE

CHAPTER ONE

Cynthia Sullivan was sitting on a freshly painted bench in the quaint village of Floral Park, a blue-collar suburb of New York City. Her twelve-year-old daughter, Emily, sat next to her, busily texting her friends. Emily had purple dyed hair, and she wore ripped up jeans – the $150 designer type. Cynthia was petting her dog, Molly, as she enjoyed the cool spring-like day.

"Emily, dear, why don't you put the phone down and enjoy this beautiful day. You kids spend too much time on those stupid phones. You should get out more and actually do things. In my days, when I picked up the phone I actually used it to have a real conversation."

"Mom please, I'm talking to Grace and Hannah about getting together tonight. Hannah invited a few kids to her house to watch a movie on Netflix. In your days, they had phones with cords on them. It's a different world today. You can't possibly understand."

"Oh, okay, dear." After a minute or two of cold silence, Cynthia timidly asked, "Are any boys going to be there? Are her parents going to be home?"

Emily let out a scream; her whole body shook as she exploded. "WHAT IS THE MATTER WITH YOU? Do you think we are going to have a wild boy-girl party with drinking and kissing?"

Cynthia blanched at her daughter's reaction and backed off.

Calming down slightly, Emily continued, "We are just going to hang out. It is a Saturday night, all my homework is done, and I'll be three blocks away. God, what is your problem? Can't you act like a normal mom and give Paul and me some space? You are always hugging us and saying I love you. Who else does that? I'm not two years old! I'm a grown woman, and I can think for myself."

As Cynthia was about to answer, Emily stopped her. "It's embarrassing! My friends laugh and tease me about it. Their parents let them stay in their rooms and text and chat all day. Act normal for a change."

Cynthia didn't let this outburst get to her. Since Emily turned eleven and started to develop, her character changed. She no longer liked hanging out with her parents or younger brother, Paul. She stayed in her room more and could erupt in anger from the smallest thing.

Cynthia often wondered if a demon had taken over her sweet daughter's body. She tried every little trick the experts suggested for handling adolescent behavior. Nothing worked!

Her eyes closed and she thought back to a time thirteen years earlier on that very bench. The images weren't as bright, and the bench was duller. The trees were smaller, and there weren't any electric cars on the streets.

Pictures of the since-deceased Esther and her daughter, Rose, were as clear as the blue sky. Esther was exactly one hundred years old and Rose was sixty-five.

She recalled the stories of their troubled lives. Their relationship and the lack of maternal love they both experienced made Cynthia the mother she had become. Stories of their lives living through the Great Depression, tuberculosis sanitariums, Woodstock '99, and 9/11 raced through her thoughts.

ONE HUNDRED YEARS WITHOUT LOVE

After a few minutes of reliving the past, her eyes popped open. Emily, so engrossed in her texting, didn't even notice her mother spacing out and the tears that flowed down her cheek.

Molly's barking brought Emily out of her trance. She noticed her mother getting up and walking away. "Mom, what are you doing?"

"Just cleaning up, Emily. Some inconsiderate guy didn't clean up after his dog. Keep an eye on Molly for a minute please."

"Yeah, so what? Let the town or somebody else pick it up. It's not your problem and it's disgusting. You don't always have to be a girl scout. WHAT IS YOUR PROBLEM?"

"Relax, Emily, you don't have to do it. I will take care of it."

Emily threw up her arms, breathed out heavily, and muttered to herself, "Whatever." She returned to her cell phone and continued her texting.

Her next text to her friends was, "You wouldn't believe what my crazy mother is doing now."

When Cynthia returned from her unpleasant collection Emily erupted. "Why the hell did you clean up someone else's giant dog poop? Nobody does that! *Who cares if there is some dog crap on the ground?*"

Cynthia's face turned red, and her expression became severe. Emily froze for a second, trying to decipher what was transpiring. *I always talk to my mom like this. What is going on?*

Cynthia's blood was boiling now. Her insolent daughter had been sassy to her for over a year now, and she never admonished her. She took crap and disrespect in stride and just reassured herself that this was just a phase. Besides, she didn't want to develop a bad mother-daughter relationship. But the remembrance of Esther and Rose haunted her.

Cynthia closed her eyes, and Emily could hear her counting to ten.

Emily was nervous. "What is going on?"

"Is she okay?"

"Is she going looney?"

Her head snapped back as Cynthia suddenly wagged a finger in her face. "I have had enough insolence from you, young lady. You are a rude, obnoxious little girl who doesn't appreciate the love and attention I give you. *Maybe I do the things I do for a reason.* Maybe I am a little *too* attentive and show *too* much outward affection. Maybe I say I love you too often. Maybe I am different from other parents. And just maybe you will be grateful for all these things someday. I'm sure there are plenty of kids who would die for the attention I give you. I put my heart and soul into you and your brother. I treat you equally and don't play favorites; neither of you lack for anything." Catching her breath for a second, she continued. "I put up with your insolence and bad temper because I love you! I suspect that if your friends are teasing you about my outward affection, they are in fact jealous! You don't realize how good you really have it. I know of two such people who are no longer with us that wouldn't mind our relationship. Let me tell you a story!"

CHAPTER TWO

"I was a nervous young newlywed walking Molly, who was just a puppy at the time. I grew up in the Bronx, as you know, and the move to a more affluent area left me excited, yet fearful. We lived in a big apartment building and everybody knew each other. Elevators, doormen, local schools, and small shops made for easy acquaintances.

"Leaving my mother and sister behind in the Bronx was scary enough. Living with my new husband, your father, was a huge adjustment also. Early married life necessitates compromise and a total reshaping of one's life!

"Floral Park was a nice area, but I felt totally out of place. The lawns were a vibrant green and gardens well manicured. The cars were bright shiny minivans and SUVs.

"But where were all the people? The streets seemed barren, and neighbors flew out of their front doors into their cars. While they weren't unfriendly, they showed little interest in more than a quick superficial conversation. There was an old couple next door that were very nice, but we had little in common.

"A few of the neighbors welcomed your father and me and made idle chatter during initial introductions. While they seemed pleasant enough, one young mother was so wrapped up in her children, I knew she wouldn't be a friend. Still another woman was the chief marketing agent for a big company and chattered with one eye glued to her cell phone. Neither went out of their way to become friends after the initial greetings.

"Luckily, we had just gotten Molly, and she became my savior. I could complain and whine like an immature little girl and she would lick my melancholy away.

"I was slated to start graduate school in the fall. Your father, being a resident physician, was constantly on call and I was alone for long periods of time. Molly was a great companion, but conversations were limited.

"I began to question if I had made the right choices in getting married and moving to this area. Your father was frequently away at work; my mother and sister were miles away and I had no friends. My days consisted of cleaning the house and going on walks with Molly. What had I got myself into?"

Emily interrupted Cynthia and asked how long this story was going to take.

Cynthia, still mad at her insolent daughter, retorted, "AS LONG AS IT TAKES! If my story bothers you so much, let's pretend it was not me but a different person named Cynthia. Now let me continue!"

Emily just buried her head in her hands and muttered, "Whatever."

Cynthia continued.

When her husband arrived home one night Cynthia was very quiet, and her usually preoccupied husband asked if there was a problem. Cynthia shook her head no, but her facial expression said yes. As he wrapped her up in his arms, she started crying.

"What is it dear? Why are you upset? Are your mother and sister okay?"

ONE HUNDRED YEARS WITHOUT LOVE

She just shook her head as the tears continued to streak her mascara.

"Okay then, why are you crying? Did you have a bad day? Did you get into a fight with someone? What's going on?"

Cynthia shook her head as the tears continued, interrupted by sobs.

"Well, I don't believe you," an exasperated Steve continued. "We have a nice house, which you decorated. We bought furniture that you picked. I bought you a nice new car with every gadget available. You are living in a great Long Island town with a phenomenal school system. You can safely walk the streets at any time. What more do you want?"

Cynthia continued to sob but didn't utter a word. After a few minutes, Steve moved to the other couch facing his wife and said, "I am not moving until you tell me why you are so upset. I love you and can't stand to see you in this state. Whatever your problem is, it is our problem. Should I call your mother and ask her? I know you confide everything to her."

Cynthia shot up and said, "No, no, don't do that. I don't want to upset her. I will tell you."

After a pause of several seconds, Cynthia blurted out. "*I feel so lonely.* When you are not here, which is most of the time, I am by myself. People here seem superficial and are too wrapped up in their own lives. I see people walking, but nobody stops to talk or invite me to walk with them.

"As I pass people gardening, they give me a polite wave or a curt hello and resume their business. I feel so out of place here.

"Even when you come home, you are wrapped up in your days' events and seem to be distant. In my old neighborhood, all you had to do was ride the elevator to meet people. They were friendly and invited you over for coffee and gossip. The doorman was your friend, weatherman, gossiper, and caretaker all rolled up into one. My girlfriends still live there or have moved to Westchester. Nothing is the same anymore!

"I have no close friends. Nobody to have coffee or lunch with. The most action I usually get is collecting Molly's poop. If I disappeared, nobody would even know I was gone."

Steve's mouth popped open, and his eyes widened. "I'm so sorry, dear. I had no idea! I just assumed you were happy in this area. You always complained about the stinking subways, noisy streets with the "L" above you. That neighborhood has more crime and violence then a person should be near.

"You always loved when I brought you to Long Island. The houses were large, separate with ordained yards. There are street fairs, nice parks, great schools, beaches, and block parties galore. You always remarked how ideal a place it would be to live, raise kids and be safe.

"I'm sure you will make friends soon. This is an established town, and social cliques are already entrenched. New people will move in, and they will be searching for friends also. What about the woman next door? I know Rita is quite a bit older, but she likes you and is always around."

Cynthia unfolded her arms, and a smile appeared. "Yeah, Rita is nice, and I have talked to her, but she is more like a mother than a contemporary. She has been married for like forty years, and it's hard to relate to her. Besides, she has her own adult daughter and grandson living with her."

"Well then, get proactive and join a club or a gym. Wait, forget the gym. With your looks, guys will be hitting on you all the time! Let's research clubs or organizations you might be interested in."

ONE HUNDRED YEARS WITHOUT LOVE

Cynthia smiled more in the sincerity of her husband showing concern and the unburdening of her loneliness.

"Another time; I'll look tomorrow. You must be tired, and I'm sorry to burden you with my problems."

Steve got up, went behind her, and wrapped her up in his arms. He kissed the nape of her neck and then her cheek. "Honey, it's not your problem; it's our problem. We are a unit. If you are sad, we are sad. We will solve this problem together.

"Why don't you call your mother? You always feel better after talking to her. Remember as she always told you: she is only a phone call away."

That night as Steve slept, Cynthia lay awake contemplating her immediate future. Steve was right. She would have to be proactive in making new friends. Now, how could she meet new people?

CHAPTER THREE

The next morning, Cynthia woke up with a determination to alter her life. She would not be a depressed, pampered suburban housewife. She put on extra makeup, fluffed up her hair, and put on her new pink sneakers. As she put on Molly's leash, the exuberant puppy popped up and gave Cynthia two loving licks. Cynthia rubbed Molly's back and said, "Who needs friends when I have you?

"Let's take an extra-long walk today and try to make some new friends."

She gave Molly two treats and patted her again.

She started up Daisy Ave. and noticed young children and their guardians waiting for the school bus. She observed that the adults were either grandparents or nannies. There was neither a mother nor father to see their children off. She thought to herself, *When I have children, I will be a full time mom. No damn strangers are taking care of my kids!*

She made a left on Plainfield Ave. and walked the half mile to town. The sun was shining brightly on this fall day and a warm feeling embraced her heart. "It is a lovely day, and I will make the most of it, with or without friends. Molly, let's have a picnic at the gardens."

ONE HUNDRED YEARS WITHOUT LOVE

She stopped at a deli to get a poppy seed bagel and coffee. The counterwoman gave her a stern look as she brought the dog into the store. "Can't you read the sign ma'am? No dogs allowed."

Cynthia apologized for not seeing the sign. As she started to back out of the store the counterwoman nastily barked, "Okay, lady, I'll serve you this one time, but from now on, NO DOGS IN THE STORE!"

Cynthia sheepishly gave her order, received her change, and scurried out. She muttered to herself, "Cold hearted bitch. Molly is in a stroller, wearing a doggy dress and smells better than you, lady. What's the big deal? I hope you step in a pile of dog shit."

She exited the store stressed, but determined not to let that little episode ruin her day. The birds were chirping, the grass was green, and the weather perfect. As she arrived at Centennial Park she looked for a bench to set herself down.

Suddenly an older woman's voice broke the calmness of the day. "Oh, my God! Miss, can you please come over here?"

On a bench behind her sat an old hunched backed woman in a shawl next to a younger Jamaican woman.

"Please, please come over here," the old woman implored. "Let me see your dog."

Pleased that someone actually wanted to talk to her, she smiled and walked over.

"Oh, my God!" the old woman shrieked. "Your dog looks exactly like my childhood Pomeranian, Missy. Can I pet your dog? What is her name?"

Cynthia replied, "This is Molly, and she would love to say hello to you. She is very friendly." Cynthia pulled the stroller over, and Molly sat on her hindquarters like a koala bear and put her paws up. The old lady bent over, patted Molly, and received two quick licks.

The woman shrieked with joy, and her wrinkled face brightened up. "Oh, my God, just like Missy. It's been about ninety years, but I still remember my dear friend Missy."

"Ninety years did you say? How do you remember so far back?"

"Oh, my dear, this body may be ancient, but this mind is still functioning quite well. Maybe too well! Believe me, it is not necessarily a blessing to recall the events from your entire life.

"There were so many awful things that happened during my time. Death, disease, suffering, world wars, genocides, riots, hate crimes. Oh, my God, the list never ends. All my relatives, friends, and husband are long gone. My two children live far away.

"By the way, my name is Esther, and this is my companion Iris. Guess how old I am."

Cynthia introduced herself and looked the lady over. "I'm not really good at guessing ages."

"Oh dear, don't be afraid to offend me; I'm insult proof. If you knew all the grief and stress I've experienced, you'd know I can take anything. I'm exactly one hundred years old!"

Cynthia raised her hands to her face and gasped, "You're 100?"

The old lady sadly nodded her head. "Yeah, it is true. I guess God doesn't really want me. I don't really blame him; I can be a royal pain in the ass."

The aide patted the old lady's hand and kindly said, "Oh, Esther, stop saying that. God loves you so much, he is simply taking care of you. It is a blessing to be alive and to have witnessed all the miracles that have occurred in the last hundred years."

ONE HUNDRED YEARS WITHOUT LOVE

Esther just removed the aide's hand and replied, "Yeah, right! Miracles, inventions, travel, televisions, computers, cell phones. Phooey! They just distract people from the really important parts of life. Family, friends, relationships... that is what life is about.

"Family units are being destroyed by these fancy gadgets. My children moved halfway around the world to get away from me. Even the rare times they visit, they are always looking at their stupid phones.

"When I was a child, we gathered in the living room of our Brooklyn walkup apartment. We played board games, read books, and gathered around the radio. I had three siblings, one of whom died at a young age.

"Yeah, pneumonia took my eight-year-old sister. I would give all the money in the world and throw away all these fancy gadgets just to see my parents and sisters again."

The old woman slowly raised her arthritic hands to her face and started sobbing. The aide named Iris put her arm around Esther's shoulders and squeezed gently. "There, there, Esther I'm sure you will see them again someday. God has a purpose for everything he does. I'm sure he has a special purpose for you. That's why he is keeping you on Earth for so long."

Iris mouthed quietly to Cynthia that this was a common event. "She always talks about the past and her dead relatives. Her children don't visit her, and she has few friends. I'm sure she would love for you to stay a while and talk. Oh, and by the way, you have the cutest dog."

Cynthia shook her head and replied, "I understand completely. I am new in the town, and I'd love to sit and chat for a while."

Cynthia gave Molly some treats and waited for the old woman to compose herself. After several minutes, Esther removed her withered hands and wiped away some tears.

"Oh, I'm sorry dear; I'm just an old decrepit lady with no real purpose. I shouldn't burden you with my problems. Everybody has his or her share of bad luck and I shouldn't really complain."

Cynthia empathetically said, "Yeah, but to have a sister die at such a young age must have been unbearable. I couldn't imagine that!"

"Don't fret, honey; childhood death was not uncommon in those days. Polio took many a young life, as there were no vaccines. It even paralyzed and almost killed President Roosevelt.

"Pneumonia was rampant in the 1930's due to the Oklahoma dust bowl. That dust spread all over and even affected people in the East.

"Most people didn't have money, and they rarely went to the doctors. My sister Gertrude died from it. Many families around this time lost young children. Parents and siblings were, of course, devastated, but what could we do? Jump in the grave with them?"

With tears welling up, she looked sadly in Cynthia's eyes and said, "Child, you are still young. Life has a way of kicking you in the teeth at some point. Everybody will lose a loved one. At first it is heart wrenching, and we don't know if we can carry on. Eventually, time has a way of healing our wounds, and the pain becomes less. At some point, our sorrow subsides, and we think of the good times. We visit the grave sights, pray that they are in a better place, and hope that we will be reunited in the end.

"Luckily, my other sisters survived childhood. Alas, they are no longer around, but they lived, married, and had decent lives.

"You are lucky to live in this day and age where we have good medicines and vaccines, and childhood death is rare. Do you have any children?"

Cynthia shook her head and replied, "Not yet. My husband is a resident physician and says it's way too soon. Besides, I am only twenty-three; I want to get a masters in social work and work part time."

"Twenty-three! My God, you should have children by now. What is the matter with this younger generation? Always in a rush to have everything; a career, work out at the gym, travel to foreign countries, and maybe, if time permits, pop out a kid. Once the child is born, they bounce back to work and drop their children at grandma's or day care.

"This is why children are crazy these days; dyeing their hair all sorts of colors, piercing all parts of their body, and texting all the time. Nowadays you see girls kissing girls and boys holding hands with boys. If that isn't crazy enough, now kids even change their sex! How crazy is that? If the parents were around more, maybe they would grow up normal!"

"In my days, us girls worked or went to school. We all pitched in, especially after that Black Tuesday of the stock market crash. Yeah, even though I was only six on October 29, 1929, I remember that day vividly."

She closed her eyes and the dogwood tree above seemed to shake softly and Esther heard voices in her head.

CHAPTER FOUR

"Esther, Esther, Esther." The call was a chorus of male and female voices, which sounded vaguely familiar. They were voices from decades past, when she was a child. Suddenly a gust of wind lifted a lone brown leaf from the ground, and it floated skyward. Another cross current caused the leaf to spin like a top. Reaching one of the bottom limbs of the barren tree, it reattached itself to a leaf bud and remained there.

"Coming home from school that infamous Black Tuesday which signaled the start of the Great Depression, there was a group of men on the steps to my apartment building. They were visibly animated and were discussing the stock market. While I didn't understand much, I did sense tension in their voices. I did know that the nervousness was about money!

"One younger neighbor was waving his hand and admonishing the others for worrying so much. 'Don't worry about it. This is not our problem! We are too poor to own stocks. Only the guys with money lost money. Excuse me if I don't cry too much. Screw them! They make us work like dogs for long hours and low pay while they get rich.

"'Remember the Triangle Shirtwaist Factory Fire in Manhattan twenty years ago? A hundred and forty-six garment workers, mostly young girls, died that day. Those young Jewish and Italian women worked 52 hours a week for just $10. To keep them from sneaking in breaks they locked all the fire doors. When the fire broke out that day, they were trapped like rats. Many died from smoke inhalation, but most jumped to their deaths from the ninth floor. Two of them were only fourteen.

"'Guess what? The two rich owners of the factory were found innocent of manslaughter by discrediting witnesses. They had to pay the victims' families only $75 each, which they were reimbursed from insurance policies. Those are the bastards that lost money today! Fuck them!'"

"'I hope you're right,' replied another, 'but this could affect everybody. The radio said stock workers were walking around dazed and in disbelief. It was reported that two actually jumped to their death from losing their life savings. This stuff usually trickles down, and us poor and common folk usually pay the price!"

Esther closed her eyes and seemed to lose her trend of thought. After a few seconds, her eyes popped open and she looked right at Molly. "Oh, what a pretty little dog you have there. What is her name?"

Iris raised her eyes skyward, took a deep breath and exhaled. "Esther, you already met Molly and her owner, Cynthia. Don't you remember?"

"Okay, okay, get off my case. I am an old lady. Don't scold me if I forget a few things. Let's see what you are like when you reach a hundred."

She whispered to Cynthia that Iris meant well but could be a pain in the backside sometimes.

"Now what were we talking about, dear?"

Cynthia was taken back as this withered centenarian scolded her aide. "Oh, I think you were telling me about the Great Depression. Did it affect you much?"

"Child, it affected everybody! Life changed overnight from a comfortable, if not glamorous, existence to a struggle to survive. While I don't like to remember those days, you really can't bury the past. Those tough times made me the person I am today.

"That night of the crash, my father didn't talk about the stock market, but I saw that he was preoccupied. My father was a big man who loved his family very much.

"At dinner he would always ask us about our day and engage us in conversation. He was genuinely interested in our lives and was always there with a smile. After he lost his job, things changed dramatically.

"After dinner we would sit around the radio and play games or read. He usually held the smaller children on his lap and bounced us as he sang songs. Unfortunately, he had an awful voice, but we loved ever second of it. We felt loved and wanted.

"Our mother constantly scolded him about pampering us kids, but he just ignored her. My parents were always so busy and arguing about things, it's amazing that they produced four of us."

Esther cracked a smile, and Cynthia couldn't withhold a small giggle.

"Anyway, two weeks later he was laid off from his job delivering seltzer to homes and businesses. He wasn't the only one; sooner or later many men were out of work.

"I remember the despair on his face, as he couldn't find work. At first he frantically ran around looking and begging for work. He eventually became resigned to a fate of being unemployed. He would sit on the park benches with many other unemployed men just staring into space. Occasionally the beverage company gave him a day of work when somebody called out sick.

"After school, my two older sisters, Sissy and Judy, sold apples on the street which we got from our cousins' farm. My mother knitted blankets and hats and sold them to the few that could afford them. Neighbors bartered items, as there was little money around. Friends in the building would give any extra food they had. Everybody helped each other out!

"That was the only good thing about those times. The true friendship and compassion from others got us through. My mother got jobs cleaning other people's houses and apartments. While we weren't rich or living the high life, we developed bonds and got by."

A smile cracked the withered skin on her face and she closed her eyes. She murmured something incoherent and seemed to wander off. There was complete silence for several minutes and even Molly gazed at the old lady. Cynthia surmised that Esther was reliving her childhood in that apartment in the 1930's. She wondered what it was like growing up during those times and the hardships they endured.

Esther began sobbing, and tears ran down her cheeks. Iris dabbed Esther's eyes with some soft tissues and said, "There, there honey. Everything will be okay."

The old lady slapped the caring aide's hand away and retorted, "Things will not be okay. I am an old, sickly lady and all my friends and relatives are gone. Everybody I loved and who loved me back are long gone. My own children never come to see me. I sit on benches and stare into space while my body and mind decay.

"You haven't lived the life I did. You don't even know me. Just stop treating me like a baby and saying things are fine. Please just do your job, give me my meals, walk me to the bathroom, and wait for me to die. I only pray that will be soon!"

The aide jerked back, removed her hand, and turned the other way. Cynthia, taken aback by Esther's verbal barrage, hesitantly said, "Is there anything I can do for you?"

Esther turned to Cynthia and appeared to relax. "I'm sorry, dear, for my outburst. Iris is really a nice person, only trying to help. I just don't like being treated like a baby. They say that people lash out at those closest to them.

"No one can really understand me. The times are totally different and few people alive today have lived in my world.

"Perhaps if I could pet and see your dog, it would bring back the good memories I used to have."

Cynthia said, "Of course. Molly, come sit by this nice lady and say hello." She picked up the Pomeranian and plopped her right next to her new friend. Esther petted Molly as she wagged her tail and looked into the old lady's eyes. After several seconds, the dog jumped up and gave her several licks.

Esther squealed in delight and hugged the little dog. "Oh, you are a dear, just like my little Missy used to do. What a treasure you are!

"Cynthia dear, if you would like to help me, I would love to see your dog again. I haven't had this warm feeling in such a long time."

A bright smile appeared on Cynthia's face and she replied, "Molly and I would love to see you again. Maybe we can come here tomorrow at about the same time. I think the weather will be fine. Does that sound okay?"

"I would love that!" Esther winked at Cynthia and turned to Iris. "Is that okay with you, boss?"

ONE HUNDRED YEARS WITHOUT LOVE

Iris, who was visibly upset by the old lady's admonishments, nodded her head without looking. Esther whispered to Cynthia, "Don't worry about her; I do this to her all the time. She will get over it."

Cynthia smiled, patted the old lady's hand, and scooped up Molly. The little dog cried, as she was comfortable sitting near Esther. "There, there Molly; we will see this nice lady tomorrow."

As Cynthia and Molly walked away, Esther closed her eyes and appeared to be napping. Several seconds passed, and Esther cried out, "DON'T FORGET TO PICK UP AFTER YOUR DOG; it is important."

Cynthia thought it was an unusual comment, but she just nodded and waved to the old lady.

With that, Esther closed her eyes and visualized that old Brooklyn apartment so many years ago. As always, the images were in black and white. Color is for the future.

CHAPTER FIVE

Before the images appeared, the dogwood tree above her started to shake softly again. The chorus of voices called her name a little bit louder and more distinct this time. "Essy, Essy, we love you!"

Essy was the nickname that her sisters bestowed her. She detected a hint of the familiar Brooklyn accent from her childhood. Again, a slight gust of wind lifted two leaves from the ground, and they spiraled upward. Magically, the two leaves reattached themselves to the dogwood and remained.

She had just come back from school that cold December day in 1929. Her sixteen-year-old sister, Sissy, picked her up and walked her home. The noise of the city disappeared as the building's thick front door closed. The familiar scent of Mrs. Romano's Italian food made their appetite perk up as they walked up to their second-floor apartment. Esther couldn't wait for her after school snack of milk and cookies as Sissy unlocked their apartment door.

As they entered the apartment, a strange sight awaited the sisters. They were shocked to see their beloved father sitting on his favorite easy chair with his hand covering his face. His color was ghostly, and they saw a half empty whiskey glass in his hand. Their mother was sitting opposite him, and her face appeared frozen.

Sissy was the first to speak as Esther just froze in bewilderment. "Papa, Papa what is wrong? Are you okay?"

Their father, Joseph Shapiro, seemed to be in a different world and didn't move. Their mother came over and wrapped her arms around them. "There, there, girls. Papa's okay, but we have some unsettling news."

Their father put his hand up and waved their mother away. "Come over here, my pumpkins."

Esther's mother, Jenny Shapiro, let go of the children and threw her arms up. "Do as your father says, girls."

Their father wrapped them up in his big burly arms and unenthusiastically asked, "How was school today?"

Before waiting for a reply he blurted out, "We will have to tighten our belts a little, dears. The beverage factory laid off most of us workers today. They claimed that business is poor as few have money to buy our products. I lost my job!"

Sissy put her hands to her mouth while Esther calmly said, "Don't worry, Papa; just get another one."

"I wish it was as easy as that, my little pumpkin. In normal times, I wouldn't be too worried, but these are not normal times. The whole country is in a financial mess; they are calling this a Great Depression.

"Uncle Harry, cousin Nathan, and several neighbors all lost their jobs. I don't think it will be that easy to get a new one right now.

"A lot of the rich people who own the factories lost most of their money and that loss trickles down to everybody. I'm afraid that things will be a little rough for a while. Anyway, we have a little money saved up and we will be okay. Don't you worry, my dears."

Esther turned around and saw that her mother was holding back tears, and she ran over to her. "Don't worry, Mama!" she exclaimed. "I'll sell apples and pencils at the corner to make money. Some of my classmates are doing that already, and they say it is a lot of fun. I'll save us!"

Her mother cried as she patted Esther on the back.

For the next several weeks, she awoke to her father sipping coffee and looking through the help-wanted ads. He went out early with the newspaper clippings and kissed his daughters goodbye. When they got back from school, he was always in the chair by the radio with both a whiskey glass and blank expression.

Eventually he didn't come home after a fruitless day of job searching and just sat on park benches with the other unemployed men. Esther's mother became much more frugal at the grocery store. Cookies, hot cocoa, and other treats were things of the past.

Her older sisters baked pies and sold them on the streets after school and on weekends. They displayed them on a small table and offered apple cider also. Esther would sit on the stoop of the apartment building, encouraging people to buy the pies.

Their table was next to neighbors who were selling apples, potatoes, and whatever else they could part with. The sisters seemed to have a good time and were often flirting with the neighborhood boys.

"Yeah, there were, in fact, good times during that period; it was just a new way of life. It was the older people that suffered the most. They lost their way of life. For us younger people this was life!"

At the end of the day, everybody put their nickels and spare change into a jar to help pay for groceries. The memory of the sound of the change hitting the jar jolted Esther from her recollections.

With sadness she turned to Iris and said, "Let's go home."

CHAPTER SIX

That night, Steve noticed that Cynthia was humming a song after dinner. It was an odd, unfamiliar song, which sounded very old.

"Cynthia dear, what is that you are singing? I have never heard that before."

"Oh, just a song I heard on YouTube. It is called 'Have You Ever Been Lonely.' It was popular during the Great Depression. It was sung by Jim Reeves and Patsy Cline."

Steve just said, "Never heard of it, but okay."

As Steve was about to ask, she anticipated his question. With a beaming smile she declared, "I met this lady at the gardens today who was 100 years old. Do you believe it, a real centenarian! She loved Molly, and we got to talk. Her name is Esther, and she was so nice. She lived through the Great Depression and started to tell me stories.

"Being a history major, I was, of course, enthralled. Talking to someone who actually lived and talked about those times was amazing. We made plans to see each other again tomorrow."

"Uh, okay, if that is what you want. But wouldn't it be better to try to mingle with people your own age?"

"Maybe, but those women don't seem interested in me. They walk around preoccupied; perhaps a quick hello, and they are off. This lady is interested in Molly and me and has real character. Can you imagine the life and things she has been through? She is a living history book!"

"Okay, dear. Whatever you want."

That night Cynthia was in the mood, and their lovemaking was special. Steve afterwards exclaimed, "Please see that old woman as often as you can!"

The following morning, Cynthia tidied up a bit and got ready for her outing. She thought to herself, *Esther is a hundred years old; hopefully she remembers our meeting.*

She put a new doggy dress on Molly, called her mother, and walked to the gardens. The warm autumn air was soothing to both her skin and her lonely soul. She walked with a purpose and anticipation of talking to her new acquaintance. "I do hope she is there."

As she approached the gardens, Cynthia noticed a young mother with two whiny toddlers occupying the bench Esther and herself had used the day before. The kids were running and throwing sticks at the birds. Cynthia just stood a few feet away and searched for the old lady and her aide.

After a few minutes, she noticed Esther using a walker approaching with Iris by her side. Cynthia smiled, and Molly started wagging her tail. Molly started barking and pulled Cynthia toward the old woman. Esther, struggling with the walker, smiled as she saw Cynthia and Molly.

"Oh, it is so nice to see you, my dears. But who are these people sitting on our bench?"

Cynthia just shrugged her shoulders and said, "Let's try to find a different bench. I think there is one around the corner."

Esther cupped her mouth and whispered, "Like hell I will. I'm not taking another step." She winked at Cynthia and then started moaning loudly.

"Oh, my dear, I just had an accident. I'm afraid I piddled in my pants, and it smells so dreadful."

Iris patted Esther on the back and said, "Dear, don't worry. Why don't you just stay right here while I get a change of clothes? It is too much for you to walk back. I'll just clean you and change your clothes right here."

Cynthia covered her mouth as she surmised the deception. The young mother gathered her toddlers and scurried away.

The old lady let out a smile and Iris smirked. Iris then explained, "That is a trick she plays to get this bench when other people are on it. I told her that it is not nice, but her reply is always the same. 'Life is not nice sometimes, deal with it.'"

Cynthia gasped and let out a little giggle. "Wow, that was good. How are you today?"

"I'm still above ground, dearie. And how about yourself and Misty?"

"I'm fine, and it's Molly not Misty; Misty was your old dog."

"Oh, yeah, I'm sorry; I guess my mind is not what it used to be. May I give her a treat? Iris picked up some doggy treats just for Molly."

"Yeah, sure, but not too many. She has a little bit of a sensitive stomach."

"Don't worry. I know the feeling. When you get to be my age, everything hurts and nothing works well. But I'm not complaining.

"I remember when I was a kid, maybe about ten years old, I knew the nicest man. What was his name again?

"Oh, I think it was Mr. Mott. He owned a candy and newspaper stand. At that time, a store like that was the center of a kid's world. On the way home from school we sometimes got an ice cream or a candy treat. You always got a smile and a joke from Mr. Mott. Men would gather in their old suits, smoke cigarettes, read the headlines, and discuss politics.

"If you didn't have money for candy, he would give us little things for free. When his regular customers were short on money, he would say, 'Just take it and pay when you can.' He didn't even write it down.

"One day, we noticed him quite upset. My mother asked him if everything was okay. He responded that he had to let go of Bobby, his worker of five years.

"'I no longer make enough money to pay him. He is like a son to me, but I have no choice. Those God damn politicians don't give a darn about us little people!'

"'Oh, I'm so sorry,' my mom responded. 'I'm sure you carried him as long as possible. Don't blame yourself. Most of Brooklyn is unemployed right now. My husband was laid off and all he gets is an occasional day of work if someone calls in sick. We are barely making ends meet.'"

"'Yeah, I know, but he was my friend as well as worker. How will he feed his family? How will he get by? What will become of him?'

"With that, Mr. Mott covered his watery face and turned away. That was the last we ever saw of him!

"Two days later we found the store closed during business hours. We looked in the windows and a few other people said the store hasn't opened for the last two days. As we stood on the corner, a fellow came over and said, 'Don't waste your time. The owner died the other day.'

"We all stood there, shocked and speechless. Eventually, one woman asked what happened. The fellow replied, 'The police aren't sure but they suspect he took his own life.'"

Cynthia noticed a solo tear run down Esther's cheeks as she told the sad story.

"Oh, how this mind remembers events from long ago, but can't remember what I had for dinner last night!

"I'm sorry for talking of morbid things on this nice day. How are you, my dear?" Without waiting for a reply she added, "And how is the little princess Misty?"

Cynthia didn't bother correcting her and responded, "We are fine, and looking forward to seeing you today."

Esther smiled and said, "Did Misty have a good bowel movement today? It is very important that dogs poop regularly! If they don't, that means they are probably sick.

"Let's sit down before somebody else steals our bench. These old bones and arthritis make it hard for me to stand for too long."

As Esther settled in the middle of the bench, she let out a little moan. "Oh, I wish I hadn't broken my hip ten years ago; things have never been the same."

"Oh, my God, that must have been terrible," Cynthia gasped.

"Well, I can't say I enjoyed it, but thankfully I had good care and medical insurance to pay for it. You know, back in my childhood there was no such thing as medical insurance. Medicare and Medicaid weren't around back then.

"We used home remedies, and if it was serious enough, a family doctor came to the house. You paid him in cash.

"Actually, during the depression there was no money around so you bartered with him. Many illnesses went untreated, and people suffered and died."

Suddenly Esther got quiet, and Cynthia noticed tears streaking down the old lady's face. She stared into the distance and started to shake. As if possessed by a demon, she screeched out, "Why, why, why?"

ONE HUNDRED YEARS WITHOUT LOVE

Iris put her arms around Esther and just patted her shoulders. She looked at Cynthia and just shrugged her shoulders.

Molly hopped out of Cynthia's arms and started licking the old lady's face. Cynthia started to scold Molly when suddenly Esther put her arm up.

"Please don't scold your dog, dear. Dogs are more intuitive than people in certain matters." She patted the little Pomeranian and received the licks with a saddened smile. "She senses a hurt in me, a pain, which I have been living with for ninety-four years."

Cynthia noticed a leaf arise from the ground and attach itself to the dogwood. The tree shook and Esther heard her deceased sisters' voices. 'Essy, Essy, come play with us.'

"I remember when I was about six years old my sister, Gertrude, who was eight, awoke with a coughing fit. My mother told her to rest in bed and drink plenty of water. The coughing persisted, and she eventually developed a fever. My mother got some pills from the pharmacist and applied cold water wraps to her head.

"She seemed to feel a little better and actually ate a little chicken soup. Unfortunately, the next day the coughing returned, and she was having difficulty breathing. A few women from the neighborhood came in and offered advice. My older sister, Sissy, urged our parents to call the doctor, but our father sadly shook his head.

"'We have nothing to give him.'

"I remember them bringing her to the window to get fresh air and pounding her back. My aunt Martha brought over some honey and mixed it with hot tea. Other neighbors suggested garlic, oregano, cabbage, and apple cider vinegar. After each treatment, Gertrude said she felt a little better and our hopes improved. Alas, our dreams were short lived, and her condition worsened.

"Sissy demanded that we call a doctor, and she would sell her body to pay for it. Eventually some kind neighbors and our relatives chipped in, and we called the doctor.

"As soon as he walked in Gertrude's room his face blanched. He hurriedly examined Gertrude and quickly pulled out his stethoscope. As he listened to her lungs he shook his head. 'This is not good! She has a bad case of pneumonia, which is going around, and it is quite serious. Why the hell didn't you call me sooner?'

"Nobody replied until my father weakly said, 'We had no money to pay you. We had to beg to raise any money at all.'

"The doctor turned and looked at my father in disdain. 'This is your daughter's life; we would have worked things out.'

"He used a neighbor's phone to call for an ambulance. My father, with tears rolling down his eyes said, 'But we can't afford a hospital.'

"The doctor curtly replied, 'You can't afford not to use one at this point. Your daughter is in a very serious condition. It may be too late already!'

"My mother grabbed papa's arm and locked her eyes in his. 'We will get through this! We have to do everything for Gertrude that we can!'

"Moving his eyes downward, he shook his head and said 'Yeah, of course.'

"Eventually we heard the ambulance siren and the clomping of footsteps. The doctor directed the two men with the stretcher toward the coughing and wheezing Gertrude.

"I remember my mother wrapping her arm around Gertrude as they lifted her on the stretcher. Tears streaked down her face. We were left in a state of silence as we saw Gertrude being carried away. Her face was pale, and her black eyes were staring at the ceiling. That was the last time we saw her alive!

"My mother and father lived with the guilt of her death the rest of their lives!"

Cynthia raised her hands to her face and tears welled up. Iris wrapped her arm around Esther and turned her head away as she wiped her own tears.

The bench was silent for a few minutes as each of the women shook their heads. Cynthia was visibly shaken. She thought to herself, *History gives you the cold facts, but people tell you the story!*

Eventually, Esther lifted her head sadly and commented, "Life can be cruel at times, but we carry on the best we can. We eventually get through it, but we never really get over it. What other choice do we have?"

CHAPTER SEVEN

"After Gertrude died, my mother's attitude towards my father changed. She blamed my father for his inaction and not supporting the family properly. After Gertrude's funeral, they never shared the same bed. The marriage persisted but the love was gone.

"My father, Joseph Shapiro, was the sweetest, most loving father alive. He had many friends and was always attentive to us children. In those days, fathers worked and paid little attention to household matters and children. But not so with my father; he was the exception.

"He never finished high school, never had any great ambition, nor was he a particularly good wage earner. Yet he was the light of my life. He always poured his attention and love to us kids. He would always give us extra things and make sacrifices for himself. We all felt important around him!

"I was his favorite! Maybe because I was the youngest or he was home more. He called me his little princess and told me how smart and pretty I was. On weekends, he took whoever wanted to go out to the park. Most of the time it was only me as my older sisters were dating and hanging out with friends."

Esther's face beamed as she continued. "Oh, those were the best times. We would go to Prospect Park. We would visit the zoo, which at that time was called The Menagerie, and laugh at the monkeys' antics and marvel at the buffalos running. When he had some money, he would let me take a pony ride and buy me ice cream.

"I would question him about spending the little money that we had, but he would just wave his arm and say, 'Don't worry; we will get by. Let's enjoy the present.

"'Besides, you are a little princess and deserve the best.' He hugged me and I can still feel the warmth of his heart to this day.

"Those days alone with my father were the best! Those were days when you forgot about the Depression and enjoyed life. I felt like a princess in my father's kingdom.

"These were the handful of times during the Depression when he seemed happy and appeared healthy. The banter was free, loving, and genuine."

"People would complement him on having a cute little girl, and he radiated contentment. We walked hand in hand all the way back home. As we climbed the stairs to our apartment, both our attitudes darkened.

"My mother, on the other hand, was all business. While she bore us and took care of our physical needs, she was a cold fish emotionally.

"She cooked, cleaned, paid all the bills, went shopping, and gave us the basics. She made sure that we were dressed properly, went to school, and did well.

"The thing she didn't do well was provide motherly love. She didn't hug us, give us encouragement, or engage in trivial talk. I often felt like we were just another daily chore for her.

"When my oldest sister, Judy, was eleven, Mom made her stay out of school to take care of the younger kids. When Sissy became old enough, Judy went to work at a factory and Sissy became our surrogate mother. Mom took a job cleaning rich people's houses and became the main wage earner. She would clean three or four houses per day, six days a week. We probably wouldn't have survived the Depression if it weren't for her.

"She would leave our apartment by seven a.m. and often didn't get home until after 6:00. When she returned, she looked like a disgusting, dirty old homeless person. Her hair was disheveled with dust and dirt smattered all over. Her clothes were drenched in sweat, caked with dirt, and stained with bleach. Her hands were raw from scrubbing with harsh cleaners.

"At first, we felt terrible that our mother was working herself to the bone. We would help her change and bring her dinner and tea. We would clean up, cook dinner, and run the house as best we could.

"Initially, she was appreciative for the help and fawning over her. She would thank us and say we were such sweet children. That lasted about two months.

"Soon our endeavors to help her were met with nastiness and complaints. Her main target was Joseph Shapiro!

"'Joseph, how can you put me through this hell? I didn't get married to bear your children and be a plow horse! I clean other people's filth, scrub their floors, and take out their trash. I clean their toilets and wash their soiled laundry for a lousy couple of dollars a week. This work is meant for immigrants and desolate people. I'm sure the slaves had it easier than me.

"'You, on the other hand, sit in the park, read the newspapers, and play with little Esther.'

"My father just slumped and took the abuse silently. As Mom stared at him and didn't receive a reply, she erupted in the ultimate vicious manner.

ONE HUNDRED YEARS WITHOUT LOVE

"'Men are supposed to be the breadwinners, not women. Oh, why did I marry you? All you are good for is taking out the trash, getting me pregnant, and stinking up the place! I came from a good family where food was plentiful and real men made the money.'

"My despondent father turned white and sank further in the chair. He appeared to age ten years at that moment. I was worried that he would shrivel up and disappear like the Wicked Witch in the *Wizard of Oz*.

"Until that episode, Mom had been cold and ambivalent towards him, but she had never been that harsh! To this day I still can't imagine the hurt he felt when his wife divulged that she regretted marrying him!

"Eventually, in a timid tone, he apologized and tried to explain that it wasn't his fault. 'I beg the foreman at the factory for more days; I look for odd jobs all the time. I stack coal for old widows for pennies. There just is no steady work out there! I'm sorry that I'm a poor earner, but I do my best.'

"Usually, Mom would just turn away and go back to her housework, but on this occasion, she continued her onslaught. 'Excuses, excuses. You are a failure as a husband and a father; you don't provide for your kids or me. You are a deadbeat and a daisy. I should have listened to my mother and married Marvin Kaufman; he is a banker and lives in Manhattan. I'd bet a hundred dollars that his wife isn't scrubbing floors!'

"My sweet dad just lowered his head and remained silent. After a few minutes, he walked over to the pantry and took a shot of whiskey. He sulked the rest of the day and passed out on the sofa.

"Soon, the one drink a day became two drinks, and Papa would try to be out of the house before Mom returned. He would usually go outside and sit on a park bench with his head down.

"He would stumble up the stairs after dusk so he wouldn't have to listen to Mama at her worst, which was directly after work. When he did return, he looked at us children with a look of despondency. He would sit down at the table and call me over. 'How is my little Esther? How was school today? Did you get enough to eat? Maybe we can go to the park on Sunday; I'll try to get some money for some ice cream.'

"Judy and Sissy would just smirk and call me a baby or daddy's little girl. My father put his finger up and admonished them. 'You girls got the same attention when you were Esther's age. Now don't make fun of her; you are all loved equally.'

"One of these recurrent episodes erupted into a life changing event for me. This time when Mama heard this routine, she went unhinged.

"Oh, Joseph, don't be lying to the girls. Everybody knows that Esther is your favorite. You dote on her more than the others. You buy her more stuff. You spend more time with her.'

"Papa tried to argue, but he was defenseless against Mama's onslaught. He learned to just cower in fear, not bothering to answer back. Seeing she had destroyed her first target she turned her frustration and anger towards me!

"'And you, little baby. You act like a two-year-old in front of your papa. You are seven years old and a drag on this family! Not only are you an extra mouth to feed, but you also distract your father from looking for work. Perhaps if he wasn't spoiling you rotten, he would be more useful.

"'Everybody works to keep us from being evicted except for you. Couldn't you beg for scraps or sell apples instead of going to school and sitting on your papa's lap?

ONE HUNDRED YEARS WITHOUT LOVE

"'Oh, what's the use? You two are from the same pot; useless and a drag on this family.'

"I felt like an arrow just pierced my heart. Even at a young age I felt the pain of a mother disapproving of me. At first, I was shocked to hear my mother yelling directly at me.

"As I stared into my mother's eyes, I saw savage rage and not a hint of remorse. She turned to see the expression on my father's face. He was ashen and lowered his head to avoid any eye contact. My sisters just shook their heads, but neither defended me.

"I started to stammer, 'I'm sorry, Mama, I'm sorry!'

"She just waved me away without another word spoken.

"I had little idea what there was to be sorry for, but I thought my mother must be right. She was, after all, the head of this house and main provider.

"I sulked into a corner and rocked back and forth, sobbing. My young mind was racing in a whirlwind of confusion. If the head of the house said those things, perhaps they were true. Was I the cause of my father's ineptitude?

"My mother turned to Judy and commanded, 'Take your sisters into the other room.'

"Judy looked up as if to ask why but before she could utter a word, Mama just yelled 'NOW!'

"Judy lifted me upwards and guided me into the bedroom with Sissy following. Mama slammed our door shut and turned to face Papa. We all heard the fight that followed.

"'Joseph, I have had it with you! Why do you coddle that girl? Why aren't you out looking for odd jobs? We are barely surviving. The rent is due in seven days, and we don't have enough money. I am working two jobs scrubbing floors and cleaning other people's houses.'

"'Jenny,' he pleaded, 'I'm doing the best I can. I look continuously but there is no work. I would gladly work my fingers to the bone. I would carry all the seltzer bottles in the world if I could. I would work in the sewers or a coalmine if necessary.

"'And why did you attack little Esther? She is just a young child. What do you want her to do? It is not her fault.'

"'Yeah, *an accidental child!* I told you after Gertrude was born that I was through being a birthing cow. I told you having three kids was more than enough and that we were barely getting by.

"'But no, you couldn't control your manly urges, and just like the sun follows the moon, Esther popped out nine months later. From the first moment I knew I was pregnant I sensed this baby would be trouble. I didn't want Esther when she was in my womb and even less after she was born!'

"I heard Papa beg Mama to lower her voice, but she continued her high volume rant.

"'Remember when the nurse handed her to me after the birth? Instead of being elated with motherly love, I felt burdened with an unwanted child. To make matters even worse, she looks just like her useless father.'

"Even through the closed bedroom door, we heard the entire animated conversation.

"That was the turning moment in my life. Intuitively I had always sensed coldness from my mother. My older sisters received more attention and recognition from her. I never saw her smile at me or sensed interest in anything I did. At the dinner table, the conversation usually revolved around my sisters. Sometimes I thought that I was invisible to her. It is one thing to imagine not being wanted, but to hear it outright broke my heart!

ONE HUNDRED YEARS WITHOUT LOVE

"Luckily, my father, when he was around, paid special attention to me. He undoubtedly compensated for my mother's absence of maternal love. He also pressured my older sisters to take me with them and watch over me. They were the ones who really raised me. It was that night where things really fell into place for me. I was now aware why things evolved as they did and my place in my family.

"Like a spear piercing my heart I was mortally wounded. To this day there is still a hole in my heart left open by that day. I was an accidental child born to be a burden to my family. I was unwanted, unloved, and useless.

"The scar Mama left has never really healed and has affected my entire life. Subsequently, during every relationship I ever had, I became overly needy and frightened that I was unworthy of being loved. Now as an old lady, I am still a burden to society." Esther put her head down and cried.

Cynthia sat there, astonished at the cruelty inflicted on Esther at such a tender age. She thought to herself, *How could any mother feel that way or say those things about their own child? If I am ever blessed with a child, I will treasure them like nothing else. To give life, give birth, and love a fellow human being is the ultimate pinnacle of life. Forget money, prestige, travel, adventure; creating life is a miracle and having someone to love and share a life is the utmost reward.*

After several minutes, Esther regained her composure and continued. "To make matters worse, I broke up my parents' marriage. It was never the same after that day.

"About a month, later Mama came home in a worse combative state. It seems she was berated by one of her employers for missing a few dirty spots on their toilet.

"Unfortunately for my father, he happened to be reading the newspaper casually in the living room. He sensed hostility the moment Mama walked in the door, and he avoided eye contact.

"Mama changed her clothes and was verbally replaying her day out loud. 'Oh, Jenny, you didn't clean this toilet thoroughly. There are still stains on the bowl, and the water is not clear. We pay you a fair wage and can easily replace you. Either do a good job from now on or seek other employment.'

"'Well, Miss Cookie Pusher, if I didn't need the money, I'd beat the living daylights out of you. If you didn't have good looks and didn't snare a wealthy guy you'd be cleaning this house instead of me. One of these days I will tell you what to do with that dirty mop.'

"Turning to the closest target, my father, she screeched. 'Oh, of all possible husbands, how did I end up with you? You are a rotten provider, a lousy companion, and horrible in the bedroom. Having sex with you is just another chore to put up with. I can't wait for you to finish your business so I can get a good night's sleep.

"You didn't even graduate high school, and now you have taken to the bottle. I am a servant cleaning other people's houses to keep us afloat. My clothes are old and torn, and my hands are red from the lye soap. I am tired of this constant battle to stay alive. In fact, I am tired of all of this. Especially you!'

"She pointed her finger directly at my father's heart. She continued the onslaught. 'Oh, my dead mother never liked you, and she was completely right. She said someday I would regret marrying you. Guess what? This is officially THAT day.'

"We all heard her grab something and shortly afterwards heard the shattering of the glass and sensed the shattering of Joseph Shapiro's heart.

"My father was defenseless. He didn't utter a word and avoided Mama's glare. He simply sulked to the front door and left.

"He was a shadow of a man at the moment. We didn't see him for three days.

"We heard he was sleeping on the park benches and drank more than he should. Every day after school, I would run home, hoping to see my papa. I cried myself to sleep for three nights."

CHAPTER EIGHT

"How could Mama say those things to him?

"It was one thing to call me useless, which I never got over. But to destroy my beloved father was unbearable. Until he was laid off, he lugged heavy seltzer bottles up countless steps and always provided for us. Even during the Depression, he would find occasional day jobs whenever possible. Was it his fault the world was collapsing?

"There were many men who abandoned their family and the disgrace of being a failure. My Uncle Max did that to his family. One day he was seen jumping on a streetcar with his suitcase and was never heard from again.

"If Mama really loved him, why did she treat him like that? Isn't love supposed to be unconditional? He never left. He took all the verbal abuse and stayed with Mama to the end.

"Sissy and Judy were too involved with their work and boyfriends to get too emotionally wrapped up.

"Sissy would trivialize the situation and say, 'Oh, they will make up; Mom is just frustrated with menial work. She thinks she is a queen and deserves everything on a silver platter. Those things she said about you were uttered out of frustration. Even though you are a little beanpole, we love you and are happy to have a little one to pick on. Mama is just frightened about our current situation, but things will get better!'

"Judy just shook her head. 'Oh, don't lie to Essy. We live in a shithole! Mom and Pop don't get along, and we are all just extra baggage. There is a Depression going on and life sucks. I don't know about you, Sissy, but I am getting the hell out of here quicker than you think. The first decent looking guy with some money will do. I don't care what he does, where he came from, or what his manners are. If I have to put out to hook a guy, so be it. Who gives a shit about love? Love is a fantasy we hear about, but probably doesn't really exist! Let him use me once a week; it can't be worse than trudging through life around this place. As long as he gets me out of this poverty, it will be good enough!'

"Judy looked in the mirror, lifted up her ample breasts, and smiled. 'Today is officially my breaking point. The tension in this house is unbearable.'

"Looking directly at Sissy she blurted out, 'It's a good thing I am a dish, unlike my ugly duckling sisters.'

"Sissy lunged at Judy and the scratching and hair pulling started. They actually fought like this constantly, but this time Sissy was out for blood. She was big and muscular with a mean streak like none other. She managed to get Judy on the ground and slapped her a few times. 'Let's see how pretty you are with welts on your face and hair missing!'

"After a minute of watching Judy getting beat up, I tried to help. I jumped on Sissy and soon all three of us were tangled up and screaming. Looking back on that episode I can now laugh, but during those few minutes it was a war!

"I'm sure Mama heard the commotion, but she didn't intervene. Eventually Sissy let up when she saw blood oozing from Judy's nose. Sissy lifted herself off Judy and yelled, 'Now who's the pretty one, big sis?'

"Eventually, when things quieted, Mama walked into the room and surveyed my sisters' tussled hair and the bloodied tissues covering Judy's nose. Mama just shook her head and muttered, "Girls will be girls. If I had a son maybe he could bring home a decent wage, and I wouldn't have this petty aggravation!'

"While Mama and I were never close, this day was another turning point. I consciously realized that Mama wasn't really a nice person. She was driving Papa away and acting nasty to us children. I would say to myself, 'Why can't Papa stay and Mama sleep on the park bench?'

"I soon consciously felt unloved at home. I never really realized until my papa wasn't there that Jenny Shapiro, while a very strong woman, was not a good mother! I started to withdraw into my own little world. While I didn't sleep on park benches, my behavior changed. I would remain on my bed more often and just stare into space. My sisters asked what I was doing, and I just nodded my head. I don't even think that Mama noticed the changes.

"Soon, I started curling up my legs and developed crying outbursts for no apparent reason. The first time Sissy caught me doing that, she berated me for acting like a baby. I remember being lifted up and shaken.

"'Look, little baby, we have neither the time nor energy to have you acting like a two-year-old. Now just stop this behavior and don't cause any additional problems. We have enough headaches around here.'

"I subsequently learned to just sit with my arms wrapped around my legs and thinking how I could get Mama to love me. I played it over and over and decided I was an ugly, stupid, worthless child. After all, Mama said I looked like my father who she regretted marrying.

"Since he was deemed worthless, perhaps I carried similar characteristics. It was true that everybody contributed except Papa and me.

"I decided to contribute as much as I could. I saved up pennies from Papa and sold a few of my toys to other children. After a month of hording and stealing a few pennies from Sissy and Judy, I was ready to be rewarded. I proudly handed my twenty-five cents to Mama as she came home one day. Boy, was that the wrong day!

"Around the time that Mama usually came home, we heard a commotion from the street below. I looked out the window and saw some young mothers with small children berating an unwed young mother. This young woman, Evy, lived with her mother in the next building. Being only seventeen and unwed, she worked during the week as a seamstress and occasionally took the baby out at dinnertime. Being scorned by the older married women, she did her best to avoid them. This particular evening, she was out early, and several women started berating her for taking her fatherless child out during the day.

"'In front of our legitimate children, she shows off her bastard child. The devil possesses her, and she prances around like a whore.'

"Evy, though quite young, was a highly spirited, tough Irish girl. While she may have made some poor choices, she was not one to back down.

"'Oh, be quiet, you ugly cows. I have the right to walk my baby where and when I please. Now please mind your own business.'

"With that she gave them a vulgar hand signal, lifted her chin high, and continued walking her baby.

"One mother couldn't endure the hand gesture and yelled, 'Aren't you ashamed of yourself?'

"'Why should I be ashamed? I am pretty and have a desirable figure. You ladies look like a sack of dirty laundry and are just birthing cows and caretakers. Men simply adore me, and you ladies are just jealous. I have an adorable baby, and I don't have a deadbeat man to put up with. I'm sure your husbands use you like a piece of meat at night and ignore you during the day. I, on the other hand, have men groveling to be with me and don't need to put up with their bad habits. I'll take my position in life over you ugly hags any day.'

"The women were aghast. One walked up to Evy and tried to grab a clump of her red hair. Evy, anticipating this event, let go of the stroller and elbowed the young mother. Blood started pouring from the woman's nose, and her eye blew up.

"'Oh, my God,' the woman yelled. "You blasted whore. Look what you've done. You're just a hoodlum and a tramp. Why don't you do the neighborhood a favor and move away. You are not wanted here!'

"Soon several other mothers threw stones at Evy and yelled for her to leave the neighborhood.

"At that moment I could see my mother arrive with a stern look on her face. She was dirty with disheveled hair but with a look that could freeze hell. She grabbed one woman's arm in mid-throw. She then moved between Evy and the yelling women. One woman tried to rush at Evy, but Mama knocked her on her fanny.

"Mama quickly berated the group of married mothers. 'What the hell are you doing? Stop picking on this young child.

ONE HUNDRED YEARS WITHOUT LOVE

So what if she got knocked up and is unmarried? Maybe she's the smart one and you married fat hens are the stupid ones. You look like shit, work like dogs, and have husbands that don't appreciate you. Evy here works hard and supports herself, child, and mother. What the hell do you hens earn? I, for one, appreciate her. You there, Miss Helen Fisher, didn't you have your first baby six months after you got married? Well, how the hell did that happen? Are you just a married tramp yourself?'

"She then turned and pointed to another woman. 'What about you, Susan Springer? You make a lot of noise in the middle of the night. I can hear your mattress springs shaking and you shrieking. Everybody knows your business, but do we harass you?'

"One of the women, Mary McDonald, approached my mother and told her to shut up. 'It's not the same thing. Both Helen and Susan are married! This little tramp is just a whore scurrying around with various single men.'

"Mama smiled at that remark and said, "Well, I was about to stop the gossip, but if you insist. Mary McDonald, why does the milk man deliver your milk inside and take a half hour to come out?'

"Mary just covered her mouth and turned the brightest red you'd ever imagine.

"'Now leave this poor child alone and mind your own business. We all have secrets, and nobody here is a saint. There are enough problems around without us picking on each other."

"With that, she patted Evy on the shoulder and whispered, 'Don't let these hens get to you. You are a good, hard-working person with more character than any of these women will ever have.'

"Evy just smiled, lifted her head high, and continued walking up and down the street with the content baby in the stroller. I heard Mama muttering foul language as she stomped up the stairs. I waited at the door with my open hand cradling the twenty-five cents.

"A surprised and red-faced mama stopped in her tracks and said, 'Now what is this, little girl?'

"With joy and a sense of nobility, I handed her my little fortune. I was ready to be acknowledged as a loveable, valuable member of the family."

CHAPTER NINE

"My grand moment lasted about five seconds!

"Mama slapped my hand cradling my honor upward. Before I could realize what happened, I saw all my change and nobility fly into the air and then crash to the floor, along with my hopes. I covered my mouth in shock as I looked into my mother's eyes.

"'What the hell am I going to do with pennies?' Her eyes bore a hole in my head as she continued. 'Will pennies pay the rent? Will pennies feed this family? Will pennies let me quit my miserable jobs? Will pennies get me a wealthy husband? Your deadbeat father brings home pennies sometimes. He thinks that will appease me and end my suffering. You two are peas from the same pod!

"'No, I am stuck in this hell of a life for eternity.'

"With that, she just brushed by me as the coins rolled around the dirty wood floor. I stood there, frozen in place. My young mind couldn't comprehend Mama's action.

"Isn't some money better than no money? It was only years later that I realized it wasn't really about the money; it was about her frustration and dislike of my father and me.

"Sissy, who had witnessed the event, took pity on me and came over and wrapped her arms around me. 'Oh, don't fret about Mama; you tried to do a very good thing. She is in such a mood that nothing can please her. She is mad at the world, and you happen to be in the way. Things will get better someday. Here, let's go in the other room and play a game.'

"That night, I just replayed that scene over and over. *What did I do wrong? She says I am useless one moment, and when I try to help, I'm still useless! Why didn't Mama thank me and give me a hug? Why doesn't my own mother love me?*

"For the next two weeks, I was in a thick fog. Mama never apologized and seemed to avoid me. Thinking back, I believe that she regretted that incident but didn't have the courage to reconcile. My father wasn't around much, and my sisters had their own lives to sort out.

"My teachers caught me daydreaming and punished me for not completing homework and being inattentive. I was told to bring a note home to my parents informing them of my laziness. I handed it to my mother who grabbed the note and read it silently.

"She smirked after a few seconds and said to nobody in particular, 'Second grader doing poorly in school. Bananas! I've got bigger problems and don't have time for this nonsense.' With that, she ripped up the note and continued her cooking.

"I went to my room and just stared at the ceiling. Even at this young age, I was adrift in a vast ocean with no anchor.

"I found some solace on my way to school one day. Something partially behind a tree caught my eye. I scurried to discover that someone had dropped a Shirley Temple doll. Although it was dirty, the face, hair and polka dot blue dress were intact. I looked around to see if anybody was there who may have dropped it. Seeing nobody nearby, I grabbed it and hid it under my jacket.

ONE HUNDRED YEARS WITHOUT LOVE

"Shirley Temple had been my idol since I read the book *Curly Top* which was subsequently made into a movie. In the book, Elizabeth Blair, who Shirley Temple played in the movie, was a young girl who lived in an orphanage. She was basically unloved except for her older sister Mary, who worked in the kitchen.

"Mary also wrote songs which Shirley Temple sang. One day a rich trustee of the orphanage hears Shirley singing and he wants to adopt her. She insists that she would only agree if he also adopted Mary. He reluctantly agrees and eventually falls in love with Mary, and Shirley is the hero.

"That whole day in school I hid the doll and kept checking to see if it was still there. At home that night, I cleaned the doll, washed the dress, and hid it under my bed.

"As I lay awake, I tried to imagine what it would be like to be Shirley Temple. That night I had my first nice dream in years.

"In this dream, my father had run away, and I was left alone with my cold mother and preoccupied sisters. My days were filled with despair and loneliness. I sat in a corner of my apartment, separated from my mother and sisters."

"In my sorrow I started to sing the sad song of a golden sparrow. At first ignored, eventually my mother and sisters scolded me for sounding so depressed. My mother would say, 'You are so lucky to have a hard-working mother like me to take care of you. Your deadbeat father ran out on us, and I am your only means of support.' I nodded my head yes but continued my sad song.

"Suddenly a well-dressed middle-aged man burst through the door.

"'Who is that angel with that golden voice singing that song?'

"Startled, I pointed to myself, and he grabbed me in his arms. My surprised mother and sisters stood frozen as this man hugged me.

"'What is your name, little girl, and where did you learn to sing like that?'

"'My name is Shirley Temple, and that song just came out.'

"'Well, you are the cat's meow! My name is John Anderson, and I am a theater producer. We are looking for a young starlet with a voice just like yours. You can be the next Ginger Rodgers or Jeanette MacDonald.' What do you say? Will you be in my play? You will be a star. People will love and adore you from all over!'

"Mother, Sissy, and Judy remained frozen and silent as this man escorted me out of the apartment.

"I went to live with Mr. Anderson in a palace in Manhattan's Millionaire's Row. I stayed with his young rich wife and three daughters. They bought me nice clothes and took me everywhere they went.

"His wife would hug me every morning and tuck me into bed at night. The three daughters took me everywhere with them and introduced me to their friends.

"I soon became an adored, popular singer with a close-knit family and many friends. My dream ended with me on stage waving to an adoring theater audience applauding my talents.

"Unfortunately, I awoke in my old little apartment in Brooklyn. My non-dream life went back to the grinding sense of low self-esteem and loneliness.

"When my father would come home, and mama wasn't present, he would gather me up. He would wrap his strong arms around me and sit down on his chair with me on his lap. 'And how is my little princess today?'

ONE HUNDRED YEARS WITHOUT LOVE

"It felt like the sun and heavens were enveloping me and all was good. I was one with the planets with my father as the sun. Oh, what a feeling to be loved and worshipped by the sun itself.

"When Mama entered the room, it was like a solar eclipse. My father's face dropped, and I felt his energy and self-worth diminish. The room got very quiet, and the air got very tense. I could feel all the unease of the world concentrated in our little living room. My chest was pounding, and I wished to be in another place as the expected fight inevitably transpired.

"The words were usually the same. 'Stop babying the little girl. If she had any real value, she would earn some money. But no, just like you, Joseph, she is just an extra mouth to feed!' It would usually end with, 'You two are useless!'

"Other times she wouldn't even acknowledge his existence and would dust him along with all the furniture. Papa spent his nights on the sofa or on the park benches during the warmer weather.

"Mama barely acknowledged my presence and hugs became non-existent. Even when Papa returned home, he was not the same man.

"My vibrant strong confident papa became an old, greying shadow of himself. A few times when he looked particularly rundown, I would ask, 'Papa, Papa, are you okay?' He would sadly smile and shake his head up and down. It was a small, forced smile and a slow shake of his head. Still, he was loyal to Mama until the end."

CHAPTER TEN

"I inadvertently became a dreamer. At school, I had trouble concentrating in class and found myself drifting from reality. Girls whose mothers picked them up from school and showered them with hugs and conversation became my envy. I would imagine myself in their bodies and spent the rest of the day being them.

"On weekends, I would daydream about life in a different country. The school library had many picture books of children in faraway places. In the books, the families and children were always smiling and playing games together.

"What if I was a princess in India and lived in the Taj Mahal? I would have servants, and boys would beg me to be their bride. I would be carried in a litter and marveled at as I passed by the commoners.

"Perhaps Tahiti, where natives would sit naked in the breeze and braid each other's hair. The boys were handsome and playful. Families slept on the floor in the same hut and were very close-knit. My body felt warm as this thought crept into my mind.

"Maybe even a member of the royal family in England. People adored the royalty, and the public constantly followed their every move. I would live in Buckingham Palace and have servants for all my needs and desires."

Esther suddenly stopped and turned to Cynthia. "Oh, dear, I am prattling on and on about a child's delusions. I'm sorry, I don't know why I'm pouring out memories from years ago. You know, I have never told those thoughts and dreamlike state to anyone else before! It's been bottled up for so long, like a dormant volcano needing to erupt. Do you want to know something? It feels good to get it out. Somehow, I feel better for getting those memories out. I'm sorry for burdening you. Thank you for putting up with an old lady; you are a good person!"

Cynthia just grabbed Esther's hand and squeezed lightly. She replied, "Believe me, this isn't a burden. You are probably my only true friend in this town, and I love both your company and stories." Cynthia removed her hand, looked Esther in the eyes, and said, "Please continue."

Esther wiped a tear, looked deeply in Cynthia's eyes, and saw sincerity and kindness. She hesitated, smiled, and continued. "People just started making fun of me when I drifted off. They would call me Oddball Esther. Oh, how I hated that name. I would get furious and lash out at them. I started screaming and developed a bad temper. To this day, I have triggers that set me off and I can't control myself!"

Cynthia noticed the old lady was getting sad and tried to change the subject. "What did you do for fun in those days?"

A tear escaped from Esther's eyes, and she dabbed it away. "Fun? What is fun?" Esther kept a blank expression and then smiled at Cynthia's surprised reaction. She chuckled. "Just joking, dear. There were good times.

"While we didn't have things, we had each other. There were no fancy gadgets, no magical televisions, no fancy play systems or computers to distract you! There were friends, family, and neighbors.

"People would pull their resources together, barter, and donate things they had and others didn't. When someone needed clothing, people would donate and give hand me downs. When neighbors had leftover food, they would knock on our door and yell, 'Surprise! We cooked too much and thought you like some.'

"Unemployed men would gather at the parks and commiserate their troubles and talk politics. Eventually, what started as another gloomy day invariably ended with some smiles and laughs. I guess misery loves company.

"The little kids played games outside like marbles, whip and top, yo-yo, and skipping. On rainy and cold days, we played board games like Scrabble, Sorry, and The Landlord's Game. You'll know that one better as Monopoly." Esther winked at Cynthia.

"Even though my mother carried the burden of stretching the grocery money, she enjoyed a successful barter or good purchase. Whenever she achieved a good outcome, her face lit up and she bragged about her great achievement to all. Her status in the family took on a higher level and she basked in self-adoration.

"My older sisters seemed to grow up quickly. To be honest, dear, they were not nice people. They were quick tempered and selfish.

"They rarely played with me and teased me incessantly because I was daddy's little girl. They seldom took me with them or included me in their big-girl discussions.

"'Oh, go away, you little twerp. We are grown women, and you are just a kid.' Oh, how I hated them during that time. Years later as adults we did became more friendly and sisterly.

ONE HUNDRED YEARS WITHOUT LOVE

"But yet, when things got bad, they got it together. They helped around the house and tried to raise extra money. They baked and sold pies on the street and once a month went to Westchester to buy apples at farm stands. They then sold them on the street for five cents apiece. While that doesn't sound like much, believe me, it helped."

"Our building developed a community garden in a small grassy area behind it. We grew tomatoes, cabbage, squash, cucumbers, and carrots. Every Sunday we would get together and make depression soup.

"This was an inexpensive food staple of the times. It was potatoes, carrots, celery, peas, onions, sausage, milk, and flour. We would all sit around the big pot and cut and throw in the foods. My mother added just the right amount of flour and milk to make it like a stew. Oh, I can smell that dish right now.

"On weekends, rather than spending money at the movies, shopping, or entertainment we played marbles, hopscotch, and card games. The stoop to our apartment building was the center spot for these games and I always won at Scrabble. My neighbors all called me the Scrabble Queen."

She closed her eyes and was quiet for a few moments. A smile erupted from Esther's face as she relived those happier times.

"One day, Mama brought home a new device called the radio. It seems that one of her wealthy clients was purchasing a newer model and they offered Mama the old one.

"While it was a little staticky, the outside world came into our home. We would gather around listening to the news, and when Mama wasn't around we put on music. Judy and Sissy would play romantic songs, close their eyes and dream of romance and marriage. I couldn't wait to put on Amos and

Andy and listen to soap operas. Oh, those were good times in a bad era."

As she finished that thought, several leaves levitated upward and she heard her father's voice *Esther dear, please turn on the news.*

The leaves jumped to a few of the higher branches and remained attached there.

She closed her eyes and thought to herself, *Papa, Papa are you there? Help me, help me, I am losing my mind. I wish I was back with you! Please come and get me soon!*

CHAPTER ELEVEN

After the gust of wind subsided, Esther regained her wits and sadly sighed. Looking out and apparently not talking to anybody in particular, she muttered, "Although times were tough and home life wasn't perfect, I still managed to fit in.

"In school I learned of a world outside of Brooklyn. I got to talk and play with kids my age. Although deficient in maternal love, I was still a living being. The human spirit does what is necessary to survive, and as such, I made the most of things.

"Believe it or not, I found contentment in my daily routines. The stinky smells and dirty streets of my neighborhood brought some security to my soul. I felt safe in the familiarity of our poverty.

"We did have nickel cinemas which we occasionally attended. My sisters watched dance marathons and went into haunted houses during Halloween season.

"For us little kids, our greatest toys were our imagination! We would use whatever was around to make games and toys. Us girls mostly jumped rope and played with dolls. The boys would play stickball and have play fights like King of the Hill. When boys and girls were together, we played marbles, hide-and-seek, kick the can, and drop the handkerchief. Oh, those were some good times!

"It's too bad youth and good health is wasted on the young! We took being healthy and vibrant for granted. Now I can't even put on my own shoes.

"I still remember that magical summer day on Coney Island in 1934. The sun was brilliant with low humidity. It was a day to remember. My father took some of us young cousins for a walk on the Coney Island boardwalk. Oh, what a place that was!" Esther's face beamed as she recalled that day.

"At that time, the boardwalk was over a mile long and packed with excitement. There was a crush of people running and frolicking around. Kids were eating ice cream, French fries, and hot dogs. Teenagers and young couples were holding hands and necking on the beach.

"The beach itself was packed with women in their one-piece suits and men in large swim trunks. In those days there were no bikinis with boobs and butts hanging out.

"Anyway, Papa sat on a bench and drifted off to sleep. My fourteen-year-old cousin, Ralph, suggested we go into the amusement area and go on a few rides. Helen and Lilly, two eleven-year-old cousins, reminded him of some problems with that silly idea.

"'Hey, wacky,' Lilly said to Ralph. 'Are you crazy? For one, we aren't supposed to stray away from Uncle Joe. Two, we got no money, and three we aren't old enough to go on the rides.'

"'Hey, don't blow your wig; I got it figured out. Uncle Joe is out for a while, and if we come back and he's awake we'll just say we went by the water.

"'Secondly, I just happened to swipe some nickels from my mom's hidden stash, which she won't even notice. I'm sure we can slip into the rides with some older kids; it's so crowded there. Come on; let's live a little. This is a great adventure opportunity and a chance for some real fun. Don't be a wet blanket; let's do it!'

"Helen looked at him squarely and said, 'I don't think it's a good idea. What if we get caught? They may send us to jail.'

"Ralph just laughed and said, 'Jail? Are you crazy? A few little kids just out for fun. Are you a chicken?' Without giving Helen a chance to reply, he started clucking like one.

"Helen got red in the face and since she had a little crush on Ralph, she squeezed his cheek and said, 'I ain't no chicken.'

"Lilly just grabbed Helen's arm and said, 'Oh, come on; let's have a gasser.'

"Soon those three started walking to the amusements and I tagged along. I turned around to look at Papa, and he was just snoring away.

"It was very crowded that afternoon, and nobody even noticed us slipping in the ride area. Oh, it was a very chaotic scene; young people were laughing, smoking cigarettes, and having a great time.

"Seeing people in joyous pandemonium was foreign to me. My world was a poor, somber place with poverty and tension enveloping us. Who could have imagined a place like this existed!

"The next hour was like being in another world with me being carried along like a leaf in the wind. Ralph was ahead and Helen and Lilly were jubilantly holding hands with me trailing behind.

"Before I knew it, I was on the flying swings spinning around in the air. At first, I was frightened by the speed and flashing images of the park, but soon I started giggling. There was a funny feeling in my stomach, and I felt the blood coursing through my body. A feeling of euphoria enveloped me.

"When we got off, Helen gave Ralph a quick kiss on the cheek and then grabbed Lilly as they giggled and walked away. Ralph in bewilderment grabbed my hand and asked if I liked it. Still in shock, I quietly nodded my head. 'Come on, girls.' He grabbed my hand and waved for Helen and Lilly to follow.

"He took us to a ride called 'Barrel of Fun.' We waited in line, but I noticed that all the people were bigger and older. Looking around, I saw a sign that said, *under eighteen must be accompanied by an adult*. I showed Ralph the sign and he put his finger to his mouth.

"He tapped some twenty-year-old looking guy who was necking with a girl and asked if he can say we were with them. The amorous guy said, 'Sure thing, kid. Just stay close.'

"As we waited, I asked what the ride was. Ralph said, 'I'm not sure, but it must be fun. Listen to all the laughing.'

"We got in successfully and went to a sitting area in the center of a large dish. Everybody sat back-to-back in a circle on the elevated sitting area. I again asked Ralph what was happening, and he whispered, 'We'll find out soon enough!'

"The dish started spinning, and I felt a force pushing me off the sitting area. What was going on? Were we being swept into a deep hole never to be seen again? I started to cry as the spinning increased in speed. I felt the increasing force pulling me into the unknown. I instinctively grabbed Ralph around the waist as I felt my legs lifting up.

"Soon, several girls slid down the embankment, giggling and shrieking. They ended up on the surrounding enclosed walls spinning and doubled over in laughter. As I maintained my grip, Helen and Lilly went flying off the sitting area, clutching each other in shock but laughing.

"Ralph just smiled and said, 'I think the last one off wins a prize. Just hold on tight!' Being pulled outward, I clung onto

Ralph for dear life. People were being pulled off one by one shrieking as they flew down to the outside wall.

"I kept my eyes shut as I felt the ride slowing and felt Ralph sliding off the center sitting area. Soon the ride came to a stop, and I opened my eyes. Ralph was splayed against the wall, and I was the only person remaining. Everybody started clapping and looking my way.

"Ralph came up, got me, and patted me on the back. 'Wow, Esther, I can't believe you won! Come on, let's get your prize for being the last one on.'

"Helen and Lilly jumped up and down, congratulating me. As we exited, the attendant gave me a cheap plastic ring engraved with the word 'winner.' I still own that ring!

"My heart was pounding just looking at the cheap plastic ring on my finger. Was I really a winner?

"At home I was a nobody. As a matter of fact, I was actually a burden to my impoverished family. In other societies I probably would have been sold off or cast away. Only my beaten down father placed any value on my existence and his existence wasn't much better. In school I was just an insignificant ant in a large nest. This was the first time I had accomplished anything and been recognized.

"Before I knew it, we were on the Steeplechase ride. I sat in the front and Ralph grabbed my waist. Helen and Lily were on a side horse, and suddenly we were off. The ride went up and down and all around the amusement area. I was holding on for dear life, but the others were whooping and laughing. I could see the crowd staring at us as we went by. I felt like I was the attraction, and everybody was staring at me. As we came to the finish line, I realized we were actually in a race and we crossed first. Ralph hugged me and planted a light kiss on my head. I turned around and saw euphoria from everybody on the ride."

Esther abruptly stopped her story and turned to Cynthia. Her eyes were bright, and her wrinkles relaxed. She appeared to turn back the clock recalling that glorious day at Coney Island.

"I know it may sound trivial to you, dear child, but to an unhappy, Depression-era kid, it was everything.

"The world changed for me that day! I saw things in a different light. There was a world outside my impoverished apartment, indifferent family, and poor neighborhood.

"Perhaps if I persevered, there were better things in my future. I left that amusement park with a fresh spirit. That was of course after being punished for two weeks for wandering off and wasting money on cheap thrills!

"Now I am an old frail sickly bag of bones. My mind is shot, and I forget peoples' names and the places I am in. I can't understand the news these days."

"They have people storming the capital building, girls are marrying girls and people are changing their sex. They have the Internet, and everybody is talking and staring at their cell phones all day. People communicate by pressing buttons on their cell phones. What is this world coming to? I belong in the past; this is not my world."

CHAPTER TWELVE

Her face brightened as the little dog started licking her. From the direction of town, a blonde-haired, well-toned young woman in a tight-fitting running outfit was jogging with her Golden Retriever. The duo stopped near a tree and the dog started to defecate. The woman was talking on her phone and making no motion towards cleaning up. Esther's eyes diverted to the woman and dog. She became silent and still as she locked her gaze on the pair.

Iris, suddenly aware of the silence, stopped texting on her phone. She observed Esther intensively eyeing the jogger and her dog. Iris muttered to Cynthia, "Oh, no; I think we may have a problem."

Cynthia, sensing an issue, inquisitively asked, "What kind of problem?"

Iris pointed to Esther and said, "You are about to see Esther Shapiro erupt!"

A totally confused Cynthia was suddenly handed back her Pomeranian as Esther rose from the bench.

"Hey! You there!" Esther screamed at the young blonde jogger. Her voice was old and raspy, but it carried its message.

The startled jogger looked up and saw Esther pointing at her. She looked towards Esther in a confused state.

"Yeah, you, Ms. Flapper girl!"

Iris rose and got in front of Esther, trying to calm her. "Let it go, Esther. Remember what happened last time."

"Fiddlesticks; let the police write me up again for assault. I don't care. I'll do some time if I have to." She took her walking stick and threatened Iris with it.

With unexpected speed she advanced to the bewildered jogger. The young woman put her water bottle down and said, "What can I do for you, ma'am?"

"Hey, lady, your dog just pooped, and you aren't cleaning it up. Didn't you notice it, or are you blind and stupid?"

The woman blanched for a second and in an angry tone retorted, "What did you just say?"

Esther repeated, "Are you blind, stupid, or just ignoring the law? We must clean up after our dogs! It is the law around here! If everybody were like you there would be dog shit all over the place. Do you want people to step in it, get sick, or mess up relationships?"

Before the woman could respond, Esther continued her rant. "You certainly don't look blind. I'm guessing you are not stupid; you probably shook your fancy behind to snag a rich guy. You probably give him sex once a week and max out his credit card. You look like a gold-digger. Or these days, I think it's called trophy wife. I'm also guessing you think you are above picking up poop. Well, I got news for you missy: you aren't any better than anybody else. If you didn't have looks and bleach your hair blonde, you'd probably be in a factory folding boxes.

"In a few years that body will start sagging and you'll look like a heap of cellulite. Your husband will probably dump you for a younger dame! You'll work like the rest of us and live out your life on social security. Now clean up your dog's shit before I give you a whooping."

ONE HUNDRED YEARS WITHOUT LOVE

The shocked woman finally got some words in;. "What the fuck? Why don't you mind your own business? You'd think this was the crime of the century by the way you are carrying on. I simply forgot to bring a bag with me. Get over it!

"Even though I respect older people, how the hell can you talk to me like that? Are you a demented old lady or is this your natural self? Either way, I don't care for your tone. Go back to your nursing home and yell at the aides there."

"Why, you preppy, pampered, freakin' bitch. You didn't forget your bag; you are just a selfish, privileged, beach bunny whore who doesn't want to do any dirty work. In my day you wouldn't have lasted two minutes with that work ethic."

The young woman, trying to avoid further confrontation, started jogging away. As she went, she yelled, "In your day the world was flat, and I'm sure you rolled around in dog shit!"

Esther tried to follow the woman but was quickly left behind. She raised her right hand and pointed her arthritic middle finger at the blonde jogger.

"If I was a few years younger, I would catch you and give you a lickin'. Don't you know the problems uncollected dog poop can cause?"

After yelling and gesturing at the dog walker, Esther put her head down and started to cry. Iris ran towards Esther and heard her whisper, "You have no idea how dog poop changed my life."

Iris collected her and escorted her back to the bench. After several minutes Esther turned to Cynthia and asked, "My dear, can you loan me a doggy poop bag so I can clean up that floozy's dog's poop?"

A surprised Cynthia retrieved a bag and went to clean up the Golden Retriever's poop. Esther stopped her, and in an authoritative voice said, "No, let me do it!"

"Oh, don't be silly. I'll take care of it; you just sit and relax. That mean lady had no right to just leave it. I can't believe how inconsiderate people can be. Plus, she was so disrespectful to you. People should be better behaved, especially to their older neighbors. I can't believe you went after her like that. You must have been something else when you were younger. I know I wouldn't want to mess with you."

"You have no idea what I would have done to her if I was able. All us Shapiro sisters were tough as nails. We had to be!

"Cynthia, I insist on picking up that bitch's dog poop." She snatched the bag from a surprised Cynthia. She looked Cynthia in the eye, and in a firm tone said, "Being an aggressive, unyielding Shapiro sister can also have dreadful consequences. Perhaps this will absolve some of my past sins."

The old lady, moving slowly, advanced to the Golden Retriever's waste. As she arrived at the uncollected, smelly mess, she hesitated a few seconds and muttered something. She eventually bent down and yelped a little in pain. Iris started to get up, but Esther just waved her off.

"Let me suffer a little and do this myself. Lord knows I deserve it."

CHAPTER THIRTEEN

That night when Steve arrived home, he found Cynthia in front of the computer, watching a YouTube video. As he snuck up behind her, he was surprised to see a black and white video on the screen. Cynthia was so engrossed in the video that she was unaware of her husband's presence. As he stared at the screen, he was surprised when he saw the content of the video. Old-fashioned hairstyles and children dressed in old, tattered clothes with dirty faces highlighted the screen.

"What the heck are you watching, honey?"

Unaware that anybody else was present, she jumped up in fright. "Oh, you startled me, Steve. I didn't hear you come in. It's a documentary about the Great Depression. How was your day?"

Not waiting for a reply, she jumped up and kissed his cheek.

Taken aback by this unusual show of affection, he replied, "Well, what's gotten you in such a chipper mood? You haven't done that in a while."

"Oh, I don't know. Do I need an excuse to kiss my husband?"

"No, not at all. I rather enjoyed that extra spark of affection. Still, you haven't acted that way in a while. Too long, if you ask me."

Cynthia looked at him inquisitively for a few seconds. Suddenly she grasped his innuendo and covered her mouth.

"Oh, my God," she blurted out. "Have I been distant, Steve?" Knowing that she had, she apologized. "I have been so wrapped up in my own feelings, I neglected your needs. Oh, I'm so sorry. Please forgive me." She looked into Steve's bewildered blue eyes and seductively whispered, "Let me make it up to you."

Cynthia fluttered her eyelids, unbuttoned the top of her blouse and grabbed him by the arm. She kicked off her shoes and guided him into the bedroom. A bewildered Steve offered little resistance.

After a particularly amorous hour in the bedroom, Cynthia got dressed and started preparing dinner. Steve heard her singing a strange song as she prepared the meal.

"Once I built a railroad, now it's done. Brother, can you spare a dime? Why should I be standing in line just waiting for bread? Buddy, can you spare a dime?"

He got dressed and quietly walked into the kitchen. He gazed at the smiling Cynthia singing that vaguely familiar tune. He lowered his head and tried to recall where he heard that song before. It was many years ago, but he knew those lyrics.

He blanched, and his heart raced as the old memory appeared. He was a young child in the hospital with his brother and parents. His maternal grandfather had just had a stroke and wasn't doing well. The doctors advised the family to pay their last respects, as he could expire at any time.

His grandmother and mother were inconsolable as her grandfather was a healthy husband and father. Out of nowhere, he collapsed and was rushed to the hospital. The stricken grandfather was partially paralyzed with drool running from his contorted mouth. Between sobs from the grandmother, they could make out utterances from the dying man. From what they could make out, he was reminiscing about his past.

His grandmother was relaying that the grandfather was rambling about his childhood during the Great Depression in which his family suffered more than most. Often times, they wouldn't eat for a few days, and they got evicted for rent delinquency more than once.

"Don't be surprised if he starts singing an old song from those days. It is one of his favorite songs and remembrances from those times," his grandmother had said.

"Brother, can you spare a dime?" As if an actor waiting for his cue, Grandpa started slurring out the words to that popular Depression song. His grandmother covered her eyes, and her sobbing intermixed with his singing. The grandfather sang that song over and over until the moment he died.

After gaining his composure from the memory of that sad day, he startled the unaware Cynthia. "Why the hell are you singing that terrible song? That is from like a million years ago. It is a terrible song about some very bad times. Why rehash the past?"

Cynthia, startled, turned around and stared at Steve. "What the hell is your problem? Why are you jumping down my throat like that? I'm singing what I feel like singing, and I'm not bothering anybody. Besides, it was not a million years ago, and it got a lot of people through some rough times. It's from the Great Depression and is part of our history. Everything that happened then has shaped everybody's lives, even today.

"Food kitchens, building projects, and even our current social security system were created. Lives were upended, people starved, families were broken up, people lived in the streets. Besides, that 100-year-old woman who I see lived through it!

"It wasn't just pages from the history books or television documentaries. It was real life to many people who suffered, persevered, and got through it. That old lady has had a tough, grueling life. Her family, friends, and neighbors came together and bonded for survival.

"They ate dinner together and talked about their days; they didn't stare into their phones and text. In many ways, their relationships were richer than ours. They bonded together from need!

"They had the fulfillment of working together for the good of themselves and their community. They had true heart! You can learn a thing or two from the old lady!"

"Okay, okay. I'm sorry. It's just that it brought back some unpleasant memories." He sheepishly sulked out into the living room.

That evening, they enjoyed a quiet dinner and talked about their childhoods. Neither of them picked up their cell phones, watched television, or surfed the web. They talked throughout the entire evening. They both relayed information that neither of them had heard before.

CHAPTER FOURTEEN

The next day, Esther and Iris were already at the bench when Cynthia arrived. Esther beamed, patted Cynthia's wrist, and thanked her for coming. "Thank you for making an old lady's day. I do enjoy your company; you bring me back to the old days when people stopped and talked. Nowadays people are scurrying and driving all over the place. They have their jobs, women's clubs, psychological counseling, and whatever. You barely get a wave, let alone a decent conversation. How are you and Molly today?"

"Oh, we are good. You also brighten up my day, and I enjoy your company. You are such a unique person. How are you feeling today?"

Before the old lady answered, she hesitated and watched a man walking his

Yorkie. She waited as the little dog squatted and relieved itself. Esther watched intently as the walker searched his pockets. Her eyes were fixated on this mundane event. Her breathing intensified and Iris appeared nervous. Soon a bag appeared in the walker's hands and the waste was gone.

Iris exhaled and appeared to relax as Esther shook her head in the affirmative. "Now, that is how you stay out of trouble!"

Returning to answer Cynthia she replied, "Honestly, I feel like crap, my dear. I have aches and pains in places I didn't even know existed. Still, you will never hear me complain. I get to live in my own house and move about when I want. That is better than my mother had it."

She closed her eyes and got quiet. The clouds covered the sun, and the wind suddenly picked up. An updraft lifted a few leaves, and they floated towards the dogwood. Like a security camera playing in reverse, the leaves reattached themselves to their original buds.

"I remember the day the doctor diagnosed my mother with *pulmonary tuberculosis*. It was around 1938. I remember coming home from school one day and witnessing my mother sitting with a wet rag on her face. She was pale and didn't even notice us walk in.

"This was very uncommon for my mother. She wasn't usually home at this time of day, and she was never just sitting down.

"She was always running around doing chores and taking care of the house. Sissy knew something wasn't right. She ran over and asked what was wrong. My mother, with beads of sweat on her pale face, said, 'I don't know. I was scrubbing the floors at work and began to feel lightheaded. I took a little break, but that didn't help. After a few minutes I started sweating and became nauseous. I had to leave work and came home to rest. I'm sure it's just a bug and will pass. Oh, how we are going to miss my wages, though.'

"Sissy helped her to the bedroom, and she slept the rest of the day.

"That night, a terrible noise emanating from Mama's bedroom woke us. At first, we thought a rodent was loose in the bedroom, but soon coughing and wheezing was the prevailing noise. We ran into the bedroom and my mother was hunched over a wastebasket, vomiting a mucous, bloody mixture. My father was ashen, holding my mother forward. Sissy and Judy brought cool towels over and applied it to Mama's forehead. We paced the floor and helped her as much as possible. Finally, after two excruciating hours, the coughing spell subsided.

"I asked my older sisters what was going on. They patted me on the shoulders but didn't respond. By their nervous demeanor, I suspected that this was no minor sickness. Mama fell back to sleep, but Papa sat on his chair in a state of scared confusion.

"The rest of the night, I lay awake wondering if my mother was going to die. Even though I harbored resentment towards her, I was shook up by how sick she was. I was about fifteen at that time, and it was not uncommon for people to die from an infectious disease.

"Tuberculosis, which was called the consumption, was still a major sickness at that time, and I'm sure we were all concerned. My young mind went to dark places as I imagined the worst. How would my life change? Would we have to move? Would Papa get a new wife? I felt guilty for being selfish and thinking mostly about myself, but I was a weak-minded child. I even prayed to a God which I didn't believe in to keep her alive.

"The next morning, my mother seemed to rally somewhat, and we felt slightly relieved. However, when she tried to do some light housework, she fatigued very quickly and looked unusually drained.

"We called her sister to come over and help us out. When my Aunt Lillian walked in the door, she covered her face in horror.

"'Jenny, you look so pale and run down. Sit down immediately, and I'll make you some tea with honey. You are working yourself to death; just take it easy for a few days. You have children to be around for.'

"Well, that night, Mama had another horrible coughing spell with even more blood in her spit up. Doctor Morris was summoned, and he was deeply concerned.

"'Jenny, you are not well. We need to take a chest x-ray. I am concerned that you may have tuberculosis!'

"Upon the utterance of *that* word, we all held our breath, and Sissy nodded in agreement. The Consumption in those days was almost a death sentence. There were no antibiotics at that time and only one in four survived.

"My mother at first refused and insisted it was only a bad cold, but Dr. Morris said, 'Jenny, we have to find out! If it is tuberculosis, it is contagious and you can infect your girls and husband. You have to do the right thing for yourself and your family.'

"From there, things spiraled out of control. From having a vibrant hard-working, albeit cold, mother to a constantly sick, convalescing, frail woman, life changed in a flash. She was x-rayed the following day, and sure enough it was primary tuberculosis. Sissy, who was in nursing school, just shook her head and muttered the words, 'The White Plague.'

"A specialist was called in, and he looked carefully at the x-ray. He turned around to the family and declared, 'You are a lucky woman, Jenny Shapiro! It is tuberculosis, but the infection is confined to just the right lung. While there is significant damage, there is a reasonable chance for a good recovery.'

"He was hopeful that complete bed rest for about three months would make the infection dormant. He explained that there were no medicines, but many smart people were working on them. 'I feel comfortable that we can totally cure you in the not-too-distant future. Until that time, we must let a well-rested, well-fed body with plenty of fresh air fight the infection.'

"Sissy interrupted and sheepishly asked, 'What if that doesn't work?'

"'We will cross that bridge when and if we have to, but there are few other treatments.'

"Sissy opened her mouth, but the doctor put his hands up to stop her. 'If after three months there is no improvement, we will explore the other options.'

"So, Mom came home and was isolated in her bedroom. Papa slept on the couch, and we weren't allowed in her room. She only got up to use the bathroom and couldn't even bathe.

"I felt so lonesome those days. Everybody was so busy I felt like a burden, or worse, a non-entity. My mother was so close, yet she was like a ghost who inhabited our apartment. Sissy ran the household while Judy stayed with friends and basically abandoned us. I never really forgave her for that.

"I grew up very quickly during that period. I had to get my own meals, take care of my father, run errands, and clean while Sissy took care of Mama and ran the household.

"All Mama did was sleep, eat lightly, and go to the toilet. We could hear her weeping during the quiet of the night. While inwardly I didn't really like my mother, I still loved her. I couldn't bear to hear her suffering so. Those were the three longest months of my life.

"During that length of time, Mama seemed to rally. Dr. Morris came every other week to check on her and was optimistic. Every time he came, Mama asked when she could start doing things again.

"After the first month of bed rest, she started to get antsy. Her color improved, and her coughing spells lessened. She would complain that she was going crazy from the inactivity and the inability to take care of the house and family.

"See, in those days everybody pitched in. Every nickel and dime whether, it was earned from the man of the house, wife, or children was vital. To sit and not contribute was like being a useless hobo.

"Dr. Morris was a compassionate man and told Mama he understood, but death was the alternative to rest. 'You can't pitch in from the grave!'

"Sissy insisted that Mama follow the doctor's advice and stay in bed. She was a big, powerful, stern girl with a short fuse, and people didn't usually mess with her. There were many a classmate, both girl and boy, that had bloody noses as a reminder.

"Papa just stayed in the dining area and chanted the Holy Scriptures during the visits. 'It is in God's hands,' was all he said.

"By the end of the second month, Dr. Morris ran a sputum test which was negative. We all let out a sigh of relief, but the doctor held up his hand.

"'This is good news, but we are far from being cured because of this one good test. I have seen this before. We are not out the woods yet!'

"That night I slept with a lighter heart. My young, naïve mind thought that Mama was cured. What a young idiotic fool I was.

"God was just toying with us. Why he does this, I don't know. I gave up on God completely after my mother died!

ONE HUNDRED YEARS WITHOUT LOVE

"Why, why, would he do this to my immigrant, innocent, hardworking, mother? While she had her flaws, she was still my mother!

"For that matter, why would he do that to Papa, Sissy, Judy, and myself?"

Esther noticed Cynthia grasping her crucifix and crossing herself as she talked poorly of God. She interrupted her story and turned to Cynthia. "I'm sorry if that offends you, dear child. I have lived longer than most, and if there is a God, he hasn't shown himself to me."

Cynthia started to protest, but Esther quickly stopped her. "Yeah, I know the old lines. God has his purposes. God wanted them for himself. They are in a happier place. Fiddlesticks!"

Esther stopped talking, covered her face, and started to sob. Iris just patted her on the back and admonished her. "Why do you keep rehashing the past, Esther? What's done is done; we can't change the past. You know that. It always gets you so upset."

A gust of wind suddenly picked up and blew a few leaves right in Iris's face. She scowled in frustration as more leaves pelted her. Esther and Cynthia were untouched.

A small smile erupted from Esther, and she whispered, "That must be you, Sissy."

She thought to herself, *Serves you right, Iris; the past makes us the people we are today. We should never ignore or forget it!*

Esther patted Molly and apologized. "I'm sorry, Cynthia. Here we are having a nice discussion, and I start rehashing horrible events and badmouthing God. You probably think I'm a demented, useless old lady, yet I can't help but reminiscing about my past.

"When you are a hundred years old, you have very little future and so much past… Why ignore it? All the good and bad times molded me into the person I am today. I will not forget or abandon the memories of my loved ones, no matter what sadness it may bring!

"I need to go home and rest. Can I see you and Molly again?"

Cynthia patted her hand and smiled, "I think you are the sanest person I know. Everybody else, including my husband, is wrapped up in his or her own little trivial world. They worry about their careers, not traveling enough, and their new electronic devices. You lived and witnessed tougher times than most can even dream about. The history books can give the facts, but you can give the feelings and emotional effects of the times. You are living history and a treasure to be associated with. You have lived through poverty, sickness, wars, marriage, and boundless changes in technology. You can retell so many things that few people have witnessed. Can we meet tomorrow at the same time? I would love to hear more of your past. And more importantly, I'd love to be your friend in the present!"

CHAPTER FIFTEEN

"So, what were we talking about yesterday, my dear? Oh, oh, I was telling you about my mother's illness. Are you sure you want to be bored by this old lady's ancient stories?"

Cynthia patted her on the hand and replied, "Yes. Please tell me your mother's story. I couldn't get it out of my mind, not knowing what happened. But, if it hurts too much, I totally understand."

"No, dear, don't worry about it. For years after she died, I was too choked up to discuss it. I never really understood why it affected me so much. She wasn't particularly nice to me, and she detested my beloved father. In a way I should have been relieved that the person who called me a burden was gone.

"The fact that she died at a relatively young age was not surprising in those days. Death was a part of life back then. Babies were born stillborn; diseases now curable took many a young child.

"Yet time has a way of healing wounds. I guess in spite of it all, we can't help but love our mothers. Even though the past images are blurred, I try to remember the happy times.

"Before the Depression, Mama was nicer. While she could never be mistaken for a warm and fuzzy mother, she wasn't the cold, ruthless domineering person she eventually became.

We even got an occasional hug and kiss from her. Family was everything in those days, and I was initially lucky.

"Unfortunately, those good times ended with the arrival of the Depression and worsened when Mama got sick.

"As I was telling you yesterday, Mama seemed to be recovering from the TB. After two negative sputum tests, Dr. Morris ordered another x-ray. Instead of the anticipated good news and restoration of a somewhat normal life, things went to pot.

"Her right lung was still infected and was actually somewhat worse than before. Dr. Morris couldn't look us in the eye and was crestfallen. He suggested we see the specialist again. 'We have to look into alternative treatments!'

"The specialist shook his head in frustration and said, 'I was afraid of this. We will have to try a more aggressive approach!'

"His recommendation was a tuberculosis sanitarium at Saranac Lake in upstate New York. He explained that there was still no medicine to cure the virus and only rest, eating well, cold mountain air, and mild exercise could help.

"We all lowered our heads, as we knew many people went to these sanitariums and never returned. Sissy muttered something inaudible, and the specialist gazed directly at her.

"'I know what you are thinking, but we have had good success there. It will take at least a year to achieve success, and Saranac Lake is far away. It is, however, the best place on the East coast, and many tough cases have been cured there. I know this is not ideal, but our options are limited.'

"'Are there any other treatments, Doctor? I know that many patients never return from those places. What about collapsing the lung and letting it heal by itself?' Sissy said.

"The doctor turned red in the face and scowled. 'That is what the stupid British do. There is no scientific proof that the treatment works, and it could kill your mother! We don't do it here in the U.S. It is barbaric and doesn't work. There is no sugar coating this consumption. It is a bad illness and difficult to cure. I wish I could wave a magic wand and promise you a cure. I am being blunt here; this is a very serious illness and people do die from it. I am considered one of the best in treating this disease. Your best option is clean, fresh, mountain air, rest, eating well, and getting mild exercise. Saranac Lake sanitarium is the best place. The choice is yours, but that is my recommendation.'

"With a look of fatigue, he folded his arms and sighed. I thought to myself, *I wonder how many times each day he has this discussion?*

"We saw him light a cigarette and move towards the office window. He stared outside and was silent for a few minutes.

"We became quiet, and I felt sorry for this obviously distressed doctor. I thought, *This guy is just as fearful as us and is genuinely upset by my mom's condition. How many devastated families has he had this same discussion with?*

"My father stammered, 'But, doc, I'm sure we can't afford that place. We are a family of limited means. I'm pretty sure I can't scrape up the money.'

"Staring out the window and seemingly in a different place, he replied, 'The Trudeau Sanitarium is well sponsored by wealthy patrons. They will work with you and accept what you can pay. If you speak to my receptionist, she can help you with the application and financial details. Many famous people have been cured at that Sanitarium.

"'Please excuse me; I have many sick people to attend.' He did not look us in the eyes as he left the room.

"Without a chance to ask anything further, he was gone. My family was left in the room, silent and crestfallen. Mother just covered her face, Papa stood with his mouth open, and my sisters were totally silent for once.

"I eventually broke the eerie silence by asking, 'Do we get to visit you, Mama?' There was no response, as nobody knew the answer.

"One week later, my uncle picked her up in his new Chevrolet. From our second floor flat, we saw her disappear into the car with my despondent father. I turned around to Sissy and asked, 'Is Mama going to die?'

"Without looking at me she replied, "It is in God's hands now.'

"I looked incredulously at Sissy. I thought to myself, *Sissy doesn't believe in God*. She had a foul mouth, never went to temple, and rolled her eyes whenever Papa prayed. Why suddenly, was she invoking God now? My heart sank as I surmised Mama's condition was probably incurable.

"'Sissy,' I yelled, 'tell me the truth. That what most adults say. You are not one of those sugar-coating people. Tell me the truth, Sissy; I am not a baby.'

"Sissy turned and looked me in the eye. She put her fist on her chin and thought for several long seconds. Tears started to well in her eyes and in a soft voice she replied, 'Things don't look so good, Essy. Prepare for the worst and hope for the best is all I can suggest. Life is not always fair, and we just have to carry on.'"

Esther turned to Cynthia and asked, "Do you believe in God?"

Cynthia, taken aback, hesitated a minute and then replied, "Well, of course, I do. I was brought up Catholic, went to religious school, and believe in our Lord Jesus Christ. We go to church regularly and obey the laws of our God. I assumed almost everybody believed in God; He created everything!"

ONE HUNDRED YEARS WITHOUT LOVE

"Cynthia, dear, I am not trying to offend you, sweet child. I was brought up in the Jewish religion, but I am a nonbeliever. The rabbis and religious zealots can say what they want. The Bible and Scriptures were obviously written down by human beings, not invisible deities. I say fiddlesticks.

"If God was so powerful and created mankind, why does he allow misery and innocent young deaths to occur so frequently? The suffering and unjustified deaths that people go through is unending.

"My parents fled Europe, their ancestral home, due to unwarranted hatred; pogroms they called them. When things weren't good, they blamed the Jews. They persecuted, drove them away, and killed many."

"We immigrated to the U.S. for freedom and economic prosperity. Yet we grew up in ghettos in Brooklyn and barely survived. During the depression we barely had enough food to survive. Our regular meal was Depression Soup, which was anything we could throw in water and call food. One of my sisters died as a child.

"The only thing that stopped the poverty of the Depression was our entrance into World War Two. While that helped end the Depression, about seventy-three million people died as a result. *Seventy-three million!*

"I had distant relatives die in concentration camps only because they were Jewish. Many nice, young American boys died in Europe and Japan fighting for our freedom. Us ladies worked like dogs in factories and raised households without men.

"Oh, I could go on and on, but I won't prattle any further." Sticking her arthritic forefinger toward her heart she said, "This old lady has lost her faith, my dear. My belief in God vanished a long time ago."

CHAPTER SIXTEEN

Cynthia listened in fright as Esther rattled on. *Oh, my God. This woman has lost her way,* she thought. *God does work in mysterious ways, but he really dumped quite a load on this old lady.*

"I'm so sorry for your losses, Esther. It must have been rough."

"Thank you, my dear; I know that everybody has losses and experiences unhappy times in their life. I am really not complaining. I'm just explaining why I am doubtful of a higher being. If there is one, perhaps he or she is not so nice!"

She paused for a few seconds and nervously asked Cynthia, "Are you disappointed at me for not believing in God? I hope I didn't ruin our friendship."

"Oh, of course not, Esther. I understand your doubts, but I'm sure God has a plan for us all. I bet that at some point that mysterious plan for you will be revealed. Please keep an open mind.

"If you are too upset to continue talking about your mother I understand, but I am curious."

Esther breathed a sigh of relief that Cynthia wasn't mad about her non-religious stance. She had offended many a person and lost many a friend as a consequence.

"Well, she was taken to a cottage at the Trudeau Sanitarium where she received nothing but bed rest, healthy food, and fresh air. We did take the long drive to visit her once a month. It really was a lovely place up there in the mountains.

"It was the first time I traveled outside of New York City. The trees and leaves were plentiful on the scenic drive. Other than city parks, I never saw forests and wide-open land. We saw deer, rabbits, and other wildlife along the way. As we got closer to Saranac Lake, the air became cooler and crisper. I could feel my lungs expanding and the blood circulating through my body. I began to understand why this might being a good healing environment.

"We were allowed to get within six feet of my mother, and she did look a little better. Her hair had greyed but her skin tone looked healthier, and she seemed to have gained a little weight.

"I rushed to hug her when she appeared in the visiting room but was stopped by a stern looking nurse.

"'Sorry, little girl, but that's as close as you are allowed. This sickness is contagious, and we don't want other people to catch it. Why don't you blow your mother a kiss; I'm sure an angel will carry it to her.'

"I looked up at the stern nurse to see if she was serious as I heard Sissy utter, 'Angel, my ass.'

"Mother cried when she saw us and remarked how good it was to see us. She unexpectedly covered her face and started crying."

"Dismayed, I asked her, 'Mama, what's wrong? Aren't you happy to see us?'

"After a full minute of tension, she composed herself and managed to utter, 'I'm so sorry I am not there to take care of you. I am a failure; I have abandoned my family!'

"Sissy angrily replied, 'Oh stop it, Mama. You haven't abandoned anybody. Believe me, you had no control over your sickness. You got dealt bad cards, which make you unlucky, not a bad person. You made sacrifices to help us; you are a great mother. You gave us life. During sicknesses you took care of us. During the really rough times you were the glue that kept us together. We are who we are because of you. You must get better and return to us. Just do as the doctors and nurses tell you!'

"We all nodded our heads, and a small smile came to Mama's face. We had a nice picnic lunch on the expansive lawn with Mama in a wheelchair six feet away. She made us tell her about school and work and the neighborhood gossip. My father remained quiet as he felt guilty his wife was in this condition.

"She told us that it was beyond boring and there were sixteen patients per cottage. They were outside for an hour each day doing breathing exercises and enjoying the fresh air.

"'The nurses are nice, yet stern. You have to obey every little rule to the letter, and getting up to walk around without permission isn't allowed. I feel like I am in prison here. I wouldn't wish this on my worst enemy.'

"Being outside with her and the family was like being on a vacation – away from the city and in the country. It was really nice seeing and doing different things, away from the drudgery of routine.

"Separation and a runaway imagination can create havoc in a young mind. Seeing and talking to Mama seemed to ease our anxiety of never seeing her again. The fresh mountain air invigorated my body and reduced the chaos in my mind.

"The only unsettling aspect was seeing my father in dismay. His guilt was so profound, nothing could ease his conscience. Before we knew it, the allotted two-hour time limit was over, and we said goodbye. She blew us all a kiss and it landed directly on my cheek.

"The reports were coming back that she was improving, and the sputum tests were all negative. We didn't rejoice or get our hopes up too high, as we grew up learning that life can smack you down without a moment's notice.

"The third time we visited was a special occasion. As we entered the driveway into Trudeau, there was a big banner stretched along the entrance. Welcome visitors. Today we have a special speaker on the great lawn at two o'clock.

"We had lunch with Mama on the great lawn, and soon most of the patients and families made their way close to a pre-built little stage. There was a sense of anticipation as to who the special speaker was. People were conjecturing some politician, pro athlete, famous entertainer, or the hospital administrator announcing some news.

"At precisely two o'clock someone crashed some cymbals, and the crowd grew quiet. The chief social worker got up and announced that this was a truly a special day."

"'Dear patients and guests, we are privileged to have someone with great courage, perseverance, and strength give some words of encouragement and wisdom.

"'If you are a patient here, you have tuberculosis. This is indeed a formidable disease with sufferers around the globe. I will not sugar coat the seriousness of this affliction and understand your fright of the unknown.

"'To family members, rest assured that we are providing the best care possible, and we are all dedicated to sending your loved ones back home in a healthy state. Our success rate is one of the best around, and many a patient has been restored to a normal life.

"'Our team of dedicated doctors, nurses, social workers, and support staff all suffer when we lose a soul. We are all in this together!

"'My pillow sheets have been soaked with tears of joy when someone goes home cured and with tears of sorrow when they don't.

"'Please let us welcome our guest speaker, who perhaps may lift our spirits. I will let her introduce herself.

"The crowd grew very quiet as a middle-aged woman with dark curly hair, guided by an older gray-haired woman took the stage. The older woman stopped in the center of the stage and moved the younger woman towards the crowd. The older woman stepped back and put her head down.

"After a few seconds the apparently blind woman started speaking in a soft voice.

"'My name is Helen Keller and that woman behind me is my savior and miracle worker, Miss Anne Sullivan. For those of you that don't know, I am totally blind and deaf.' She paused a few moments, and the crowd buzzed and a few started to clap.

"'I have not had an easy life and was suicidal early on. Through the help of many dedicated people, I have learned, and can do, many things. I have written books, graduated Radcliff College cum laude, and now give motivational speeches. I would never have made it here – or for that matter, anywhere – without the help of some very dedicated people.

"'In 1888, Dr. Alexander Graham Bell sent me to the Perkins Institute for the Blind in Boston. It was there that I was mentored and saved by this remarkable woman behind me.'

Miss Anne Sullivan remained motionless with her head still lowered. 'Through painstaking slow and persistent prodding, she somehow got me to associate objects with words. You have no idea how hard she worked and the persistence involved in the process."

"The odds of success were slim, and I gave up many times. She somehow brought me back when I gave up. Because of this miracle worker, I have led a tough but fulfilling life despite bad circumstances.

"'But my reason for being here today is not to talk about myself. My hope is to provide inspiration to the members of this community. Even though I cannot see the sun, I can feel its warmth and smell the clean fresh air. Many people think that because I cannot see or hear, I am shut out from all the brightness and beauty of the world. This is not true!

"'Life has many pleasures for me. The smell of the flowers, the love of children, my work, and my books are my joy."

"I think of my limitations as a key, which has opened many closed doors. My other senses are heightened, and I can help others with disabilities by my writings and advocacies.

"'From my experiences, I can truly say that happiness dwells in the heart, and outward circumstances cannot take it away from us. Many people think that their own misfortune is the greatest misfortune possible. That is a very selfish view to take. There is always somebody much worse than ourselves.

"'I have learned to live with my afflictions and make the most of my other abilities. While the journey has been long and tedious, with disappointments along the way, the rewards make it all worthwhile.'"

"While I do not have the same ailments of this community, we all share hardships. I encourage all of you to not lose hope, not to give into despair, and prepare yourself for the long haul.

"'Don't be afraid to lean on others and love your family and friends. Though we might not win the war, we can win battles and live our life to the fullest.

"'There is no death that does not come from a life!'"

The old Esther faltered and hesitated. She shook her head and turned to Cynthia. "Oh, the address was more involved and orated more eloquently than this senile brain can remember.

"I can tell you this though: families of the afflicted stood up and clapped. Some wiped away tears and turned to their afflicted family member. Many of the sick smiled, and you could sense a feeling of hope swirling around them."

"As my mother's face lit up and my father smiled, a nearby agitator interrupted the proceedings. From close by, a young familiar female voice shouted out, 'Bull crap!'

"The crowd in wonder and my family in horror turned towards the agitator. My father covered his face, and my mother clasped her own head in embarrassment. The troublemaker was my own sister, Sissy!

"Luckily, Miss Keller couldn't hear the dissent from my own disgruntled sister. We all heard angry insults from some nearby audience members and demands to be quiet.

"Sissy defiantly yelled back, 'Ms. Goody Two Shoes is describing a fantasy world. There is no sugar coating TB. You can feel good from her talk all you want, but that doesn't change reality.'

"The aghast audience, who seconds ago had hope in their hearts, got ghostly quiet. I observed Anne Sullivan tap Miss Keller on the shoulder, and she stopped talking.

"I don't know what got into me, but I then did something I never did before or after. I raised my hand and slapped Sissy with a sound that all but Miss Keller heard."

ONE HUNDRED YEARS WITHOUT LOVE

"As we both recoiled from the shock of my attack, I yelled at her to shut up. I guess the voice of hope being thwarted by the voice of gloom pushed me over the edge.

"Sissy, while shocked, quickly recovered and pushed me to the ground. I got up and tried to push her back, but she was too strong. She laughed at my useless attack, tossed me to the ground, and jumped on top of me.

"We rolled around on the ground for a few seconds, but I was like a blade of grass in her way. As she pinned my arms down and put all her weight on me, she asked, 'Now why did you hit me, little sis?'

"I tried to spit in her face but ended up with my own slobber running down my chin. In a low voice I hissed, 'Why do you have to be so negative all the time? You embarrassed us, and most importantly, you dashed Mom's spirits. Here you have a famous handicapped person giving hope and faith to all of us. Miss Keller has lived the toughest of lives and is an inspiration. Did you see Mama and Papa's faces light up as she spoke? When was the last time you saw that? Why did you have to ruin the moment?'

"Sissy lifted me up and pushed me to the side of a cottage. 'Listen, you little jellybean, let me tell you a few facts of life.

"'Just because the famous Helen Keller says thing will be alright, doesn't alter the facts. Mama is very sick and may never leave this place. Papa is out of work and a very depressed man. We are lucky he doesn't abandon us and become a hobo like Uncle Manny. We lost our sister, Gertrude, when she was only eight years old. We live in a tenement and struggle to put food on the table and pay the rent. Judy got married and moved upstate. She doesn't love her husband; he was just a one-way ticket out the house. Life is a brutal struggle to survive, and few people are truly happy. Now just grow up and face the real world, little sis!'

"I stared into her glaring eyes, and all I saw was the blackness of her pupils and her soul. Deep down, I suspected she was never really happy and was jealous of Judy and myself. Even though she eventually married, she was always a bitter, disgruntled person.

"While many patients and their families left that afternoon uplifted, I cried myself to sleep that night and many more. This was not a small, trivial catfight. She dashed my hope, dreams, and young innocence with cold reality."

Esther's voice grew weak, and she barely finished her last sentence. She put her head down, started crying, and murmured, "Mama, I'm sorry for your suffering. While you may not have treated me the best, you are still my mother. You deserved better! I'm sure under different circumstances you would have been nicer to me. Even though I will never forget your emotional abandonment of me, you will always be my mother!"

CHAPTER SEVENTEEN

This autumn day was much colder than the previous, and Iris bundled Esther up. Iris insisted that it was too cold for Esther to be out, but the old lady was adamant.

"Oh, Poppy seeds! Stop treating me like an old lady! I want to see my friends, Cynthia and Molly."

Iris just threw her arms up and muttered, "Okay. It's your funeral, Esther. Do as you like."

"Yeah, it will be my funeral soon enough. Let me enjoy what time I have left." Esther turned to Cynthia and said, "I'm sorry about yesterday, my dear. It seems I always end up bawling in front of you. You are such a kind person for putting up with this old lady. I wish I could do something for you and your sweet dog!

"Oh, and what a precious little dog you are." She patted the pampered Pomeranian and received a lick in return. Esther said, "I would love if the afterlife consisted of dogs licking me continuously."

Cynthia replied, "Believe me, I enjoy our time together. You are a genuine friend with true character and are a joy to be with. I truly look forward to our time together.

"Besides that, you are an amazing person! You remind me of Helen Keller. While I have only heard of her, you have actually seen her and heard her speak. You have lived and witnessed so much. You have experienced excessive hardships and survived. You are my inspiration.

"If it doesn't upset you too much, I'd like to hear what happened to your mother." Cynthia lowered her voice and asked timidly, "Did she die at the sanatorium?"

Esther took a deep breath, and like a vacuum cleaner sucking up dirt, several leaves arose and attached themselves to the tree.

"Well, Mom did make it out of the sanitarium. After a year of being stuck in that place, she did come home. The sanatorium did in fact have dedicated doctors, nurses and social workers, but it was still hell.

"Patients were constantly coughing, running fevers, and wasting away. It wasn't really living; it was hanging on. I think most doctors sent people there to protect others. I guess I can't really blame them.

"Perhaps the worst way to die is from tuberculosis. My mother would tell us that when a lung was extremely damaged by the disease, it would literally explode. Blood was vomited and the patient died soon afterwards.

"A few times during our visits, a previously occupied bed was empty. When we dared to ask where the person was, Mom would shake her head and not answer. Occasionally she would brighten up and say that the person went home and was cured.

"Fiddlesticks. They may have made it out alive, but they were never really cured. The disease would resurface years later, and they eventually died from it.

"Anyway, after about a year Mom was better, and her sputum tests were negative. An x-ray showed that her lung was significantly damaged, but there was no sign of any active infection.

ONE HUNDRED YEARS WITHOUT LOVE

"She was declared 'restored to health' and was sent home.

"We hung a 'welcome home' sign across the doorway, and several relatives came over. Surprisingly, other close relatives and friends stayed away.

"Once you have been a TB patient, people still believe you can infect them. My mother and the rest of us carried that stain with us for years.

"Some of my friends kept their distance and would seem to avoid me. Mama's previous best friends became scarce, and we felt somewhat abandoned. Sissy cursed and badmouthed all the fair weathered friends. It got so bad that Papa looked for a new place to live where nobody knew us.

"We found a new place in Williamsburg, Brooklyn, which was not as nice, and one bedroom fewer. Since Judy had gotten married and moved upstate, there wasn't the need for a large place anyway. It took several trips to move all our things and only a few neighbors bade us farewell. With tears in our eyes, we left our home of over twenty years."

"We soon got to know our new neighbors who knew nothing about Mom's TB. I would explore the new stores and family newsstands with Sissy and found a new world to explore. People seemed more open to strangers and treated us with kindness and respect.

"A few of my new classmates started talking about boys, and I found my interests changing. I had my hair straightened and started using some cheap lipstick. My figure started filling out and I gained weight in all the right places. My mother noticed the changes, shaking her head in disapproval but saying nothing.

"A few boys started talking to me, and I noticed them staring at me when they thought I wasn't looking. I asked a few girlfriends what they were looking at, and they just giggled. 'Esther Shapiro, you are a sixteen-year-old pretty girl with a curvy figure. That's what they are looking at!'

"A smile came to my face unexpectedly. I felt a warm flush and my mind felt lighthearted. Other than my dear father, this was the first time people held me in admiration. I spent the rest of the day floating on the clouds after finally achieving some adoration.

"For the next month, I felt good about myself, believing people loved me for me. One weekend, I was shopping with Sissy and was in an extra good mood. Sissy had noticed my recent change in demeanor and asked, 'Essy, why have you been so cheerful lately?'

"'Oh, I don't know. Perhaps it is the change in scenery and my new school. I seem to have made some nice friends and guess what? Boys seem to be interested in me."

"Sissy smirked and gave a haughty laugh. 'Oh, little sister, you are the age when boys become attracted to young girls. Boys and men are different from girls. Their hormones are out of control, and they want a woman's body.

"'The same thing happened to me about your age, and I am an ugly duckling. I have been propositioned and have slapped many a groping hand.

"'You are much prettier than me and you fill out your outfits very well. That's why the boys are interested in you. Girls, for that matter, like to hang out with attractive girls too.'"

"I got so mad at her that I shrieked out, 'God damn you, Sissy! They like me because of who I am and not because I have some breasts and a butt! And what makes you an authority on such things anyway? You don't have a boyfriend or even date that much.'

ONE HUNDRED YEARS WITHOUT LOVE

"'Well, everybody knows these things. If I had your looks and didn't weigh so much, the buzzards would be all over me. Even still, sometimes when I leave work or walk home late at night, I get catcalls and requests for a romp in the park. I have heard so many crude remarks, it would make you cringe. Almost everybody I have dated couldn't wait to put their hands up my skirt. When you have a woman's body, men want you!'

"Knocked off my pedestal slightly, I retorted, 'Well, what about Mama and Papa? They've been married forever! Now that has to be true love.'

"'I hate to break the news to you, little sis, but Judy was born six months after they got married. Do the math, little girl!'

"After a few calculations, I covered my face in horror.

"Sissy just smiled and said, 'The world is shit, and we are just tumbleweeds being blown around. Maybe you'll land in a good spot, maybe you won't. The world is meant for the tough that can roll with the wind. If you aren't prepared, you will get blown around and land in shit!'

"I didn't utter a word the rest of the day. I walked around in confusion. Was I suddenly popular and worthwhile because of my changing physical appearance?

"I wondered to myself that night, whether Sissy was telling the truth or just bitter from the hand she had been dealt? On the one hand, I remembered what Helen Keller had said that faraway afternoon at the sanatorium. Happiness dwells from the heart and not outward circumstances.

"Yet how can the heart be happy when outside circumstances are terrible? Mom wasn't herself, we had to move, my father was depressed, Judy moved away, and Sissy insisted people were interested in me for only one reason.

SANDER M. LEVINE

"Who was right? Was it the hard and bitter Sissy or the blind and deaf optimist Helen Keller?"

CHAPTER EIGHTEEN

The next day, Esther and Iris were not at the park. Cynthia apprehensively paced and waited around for an hour. Molly started crying as she looked around for Esther and Iris. "Molly, I can't imagine where they are. I hope Esther is okay."
Several more days passed and still no Esther or Iris. Exactly one week to the day she last saw Esther, Cynthia and Molly gave it one last try.

A woman Cynthia had never seen before was sitting on their bench with her head down, wiping away tears. As Cynthia walked by, wondering if she'd ever see Esther again, Molly unexpectedly jumped towards the strange woman on the bench.

Cynthia yanked on the Pomeranian's leash and admonished her. In a strangely familiar voice, the woman looked up and said, "Oh, please don't yell at your sweet little dog. She didn't bother me at all. As a matter of fact, my mother loves Pomeranians, and so do I. Is your name Cynthia and is this Molly?"

Taken aback by this unfamiliar woman knowing both her and Molly's names, she didn't know how or if to respond. How could this woman know who she was? While there was some familiarity in her accent, Cynthia was sure they had never previously met.

"Oh, don't look so frightened; I am a harmless creature who may in fact know you. My name is Rose, and I am Esther Shapiro's daughter. She has spoken so much about you that I feel like we are already acquaintances."

Cynthia shook her head in acknowledgement but was still too shocked to say anything.

"Won't you sit down for a while?" Rose slid over to make some room and in a low voice uttered, "I have some unpleasant news about my mother." Cynthia, still surprised about this encounter, sat down and quietly waited for the news of Esther's' passing.

For a few moments, Rose was quiet and just patted Molly, who welcomed the attention. Staring at the quiet daughter of Esther, Cynthia peered into the face of a sorrowful soul.

She had grey, disheveled hair and dark circles under her eyes. It didn't look like a drop of make up or a hairbrush had touched that head in a long time. Frown lines were prominent, and her left upper eyelid was droopy. Her shirt and pants were dark, ill-fitting, and wrinkled. She could have been mistaken for a homeless person.

After a few moments and a few dabs of her eyes, Rose started her story. "Mom has pneumonia and is bedridden. I am her only daughter, although I'm sure she never mentioned me. I do have a brother in California, John, who hasn't seen mom in over twenty years. Why that is, I don't know; he used to be her favorite.

"I flew in from Chicago when Iris informed me of her condition, which is not good. Mom asked if I could find you and convey her best wishes and apologize for not meeting you."

Cynthia, feeling a little more relaxed, responded, "Oh, dear. I am so sorry to hear that she is so sick. I was afraid of something like that. I have been coming here every day for the past week looking for her. In the short time that I have known her, we have become quite close. She is such a nice woman, and I enjoy her company. She is one of the few friends I have made here."

"Why don't you sit for a while with your pretty little dog. It is such a nice day and Mom encouraged me to chat with you. She says such nice things about you. She even said you were like a granddaughter to her."

As Rose uttered that last statement, she put her head down and started sobbing.

Cynthia patted Rose on the shoulder and tried to comfort this new acquaintance's anguish. She said, "I'm sure your mother will recover; she is a very strong-willed woman! She has overcome worse things than a little pneumonia."

Rose just put her hands in front of her face in defense. "The cause of my tears is not really about my mother's grave health. She has led a long, healthy life and is in fact one hundred years old. All her friends are gone, all relatives except her reclusive son and her estranged daughter, who by the way, is me, are also dead. Every bone in her body aches, and perhaps it is for the best that her suffering ends.

"I know it sounds mean, but we don't live forever, and she may be happier in the afterlife."

Cynthia, sensing depth and despair in this woman, moved slightly closer to Rose. She scooped up Molly and hesitantly asked, "Will your mother make it?"

"The doctors aren't optimistic, to tell you the truth. She is quite weak, and her lungs are still congested, despite the antibiotics. She is receiving intravenous fluids and painkillers to make her more comfortable. It's probably just a matter of time.

"She seems to be losing her spirit but also seems at peace. She has had such a long, tough life, perhaps it's for the best."

Cynthia just nodded her head and responded, "Yeah, I've heard some of the details. You must be proud of the tough times and adversities that your mother has endured and overcome. I bet she was a real tigress when she was younger!"

Rose rolled her eyes at this last comment. "Boy, that is an understatement! As a child, young woman, wife, mother, you name it. She is hell on wheels! I see you got to know my mother pretty well; she is one tough cookie."

Rose paused, took a deep and long breath and unburdened herself. "To tell you the truth, Mom and I were never really close. She rarely talked about her past, or for that matter, growing up in tough times. Whatever my brother and I learned about our mother's past was secondhand or by eavesdropping. My aunts Sissy and Judy and Mom would get together occasionally.

"Sissy was widowed and lived in Queens while we were kids. She came over frequently and was very nice to John and me. She had a potty mouth that you wouldn't believe. She had no secrets and could curse, swear, and confront people like few others. We loved her and cherished her visits. She in turn loved us and would do anything to help out.

"She was a hefty woman and tough as nails. She could do the undoable and never back down from a confrontation. If you needed help, there was nobody more helpful. If you rubbed her the wrong way, she was your worst enemy!

"She would gossip about friends, relatives, and neighbors in a derogatory way. She seemed to dwell on the bad qualities of people and life. I rarely heard her laugh or discuss nice things. It was always, 'asshole politician,' or 'nasty neighbors,' and so on. Yet, somehow, she was fun to be with and always brought us presents and talked to us as equals. I loved her honesty and brazenness.

"Since my own mother barely acknowledged my existence, she was my confidant and role model. She bought me my first bra, taught me about menstrual periods, and everything to know about dating. If somebody bullied or treated me poorly, they would answer to Aunt Sissy. The harassment ended immediately!

"Aunt Judy, the oldest Shapiro sister, lived upstate and would visit occasionally with her husband. Uncle Ray was nice enough, but boring as hell! He didn't talk much and played chess by himself. He would sit on the porch, smoke, and made disgusting noises trying clear his throat. John and I would cover our ears to tune out those constant 'ahems.'

"Aunt Judy, in contrast to Aunt Sissy, acted like a queen boasting to her common folk relatives. She would babble on about her nice house, her cruises, and social events. While she was socially nice to John and me, it was never really close. Sissy and Mom would grin and bear her haughty talk but cringed as the incessant prattle continued on.

"After an hour of small talk, things would invariably escalate. Like a recurring dream, a distant past event was brought up. The nice little Shapiro sister get together quickly turned ugly! I remember vividly one of the worst of these episodes.

"Sissy brought up a memory of how she did all the house preparation this one particular Thanksgiving Day when some relatives visited. Despite all her efforts, people weren't satisfied.

"Judy retorted that everybody worked hard that day, and it was just her imagination. Judy couldn't resist adding that they all had it rough in those days and Sissy was just a bitter, unhappy city dweller.

"Mom, the youngest, was quiet until their mother and father were mentioned. When either of them was brought up, Mom just looked down and turned red. You could see her tense up and start to shake. After a few seconds of unsuccessful restraint, she joined the battle!

"She suddenly yelled, 'Just shut the hell up! Why don't you two just let the past go! We lived through the Great Depression, our mother got TB, and our younger sister died because we were so poor!'

"'Why do you always go back to the bad times? Even when you do, it's about trivial things like ex-boyfriends or petty jealousy.'

"Mom imitated Judy and said, 'Oh, I'm so pretty,' and primped her hair. Then she imitated Sissy by sticking her chest out and showing cleavage. 'But I got bigger boobs than you do, and boys just can't take their eyes off them.'

"Back in her usual voice she continued, 'You don't regret Papa's abuse from Mom! She treated him like dirt when he couldn't support us. What about the forever love a married couple is bonded to, in good and bad times? He used to sleep on park benches to avoid Mom. His head was always down, knowing that he wasn't the breadwinner. Did Mom try to lighten his woes?'

"Not waiting for an answer, she continued, 'No! Instead, she piled on his bad circumstance with constant demeaning and verbal abuse. Still he hung by our side and loved and cared for us the best he could. He took care of Mom when she was sick and frail and never took another woman. Yet, she never apologized for making his life miserable, or for that matter, not showing him an ounce of love. She demeaned him until the day she died!'

ONE HUNDRED YEARS WITHOUT LOVE

"'Oh, shut the hell up,' interrupted Sissy. 'You are only saying that because you were Papa's favorite. The two of you were like peas in a pod. You stood by as the world was crumbling around us. Yeah, Mom yelled at Pop, but why not? He could have hustled more and begged, borrowed, or stolen to keep us afloat. Mom worked her ass off, working two jobs, cleaning, cooking, and grocery shopping. Did Papa ever try to help maintain the house at least? No! He sat on park benches talking, smoking, and drinking with the other useless unemployed men. He undoubtfully sent Mom to an early grave.'

"Suddenly John and I heard a shrieking, animal-like noise. We heard the crash of a lamp hitting the floor and glass shattering. Cursing, scuffling, and fighting ensued. Not knowing what to do, John and I ventured into the living room to a startling sight.

"Our petite hundred-pound mom had Aunt Sissy on the ground and was ripping hair from her head. Aunt Judy, in turn, was screaming and trying to pull mom off of Sissy. The Worldwide Wrestling Community would have paid a fortune for this event!

"As they were locked in battle, both screaming and bleeding, Aunt Judy jumped on top of both of them. Mom was knocked clear off Aunt Sissy with a clump of hair as a souvenir. She was crying and screaming as she flew through the air. Blood oozed from scratches to her face.

"Aunt Sissy, being relieved of our mom on top of her, punched Aunt Judy in the stomach, thinking she'd been attacking her too. Aunt Judy let out a loud grunt as she absorbed the blow. She gasped for air as she held her rib cage and moaned in agony. She staggered to a chair, bent over, and vomited her lunch.

"Aunt Sissy had a black eye where our dainty mom had punched her and a bald spot where mom had ripped out some hair. Our mother was bleeding from facial scratches, which were so deep they needed to be stitched up. Aunt Judy had two broken ribs courtesy of Aunt Sissy's right hand. Needless to say, the hospital emergency room was busy that day.

"This is how John and I picked up information about their lives. I know they had tough times during the Depression, I know my grandmother died from TB, I know she lost a sister in childhood, but little besides that.

"It was obvious that family dynamics shaped their entire lives and attitudes. Whatever occurred in their childhood, they maintained throughout their lives in a bitter manner. They took that bitterness to the grave."

CHAPTER NINETEEN

"The few times we directly asked about her past family life, Mom would start a story, but inadvertently, she would arrive at a bad or depressing part and end abruptly. She would say, 'I don't want to talk about it anymore.' After a while, we stopped asking.

"It didn't really help that our father died suddenly at a young age. While not a perfect marriage, she was content and had children. She seemed gratified to have a stable family, live in a nice house, and have friends.

"Still, she had a temper that erupted more often than most. Our father could calm her down, but still, neighbors and friends witnessed many a tumultuous episode of intense anger and poor self-control.

"Her wild, nasty temper got worse after my father's death. While people were still nice, couple friendships withered. Acquaintances aware of her volatile temperament would become strangers. She became lonely and overwhelmed from single motherhood and being the sole breadwinner. She struggled in this new capacity, and depression became her new companion.

"Luckily, Aunt Sissy helped out and got her through. Aunt Sissy, being widowed herself, became friendlier, and they formed a tumultuous bond. They got into occasional spats with short periods of separation, yet they always resolved their quarrels. They remained friends and confidants until Aunt Sissy died in ninety-nine.

"While she was helpful, she was also critical of my mom's inability to cope. She would chide my mother for not being self-sufficient.

"'Papa always babied you and now you are still childlike. You need to grow up and take charge. There is no one here to protect you now!'

"Mom was defenseless at Aunt Sissy's admonishments and often broke down. Sissy would apologize but tell her it was for her own good. 'Life can be rough, and you must be tougher. Don't forget you have children to take care of now.'

"Sometimes in the middle of the night we would hear her cry, 'Why? Why? I finally found fulfillment and you took it away from me. Why? Why?' She was never really the same after my father died.

"Perhaps if her time is near, my parents will be reunited, and she can be happy again."

Cynthia sensed that Rose possessed many regrets and a life full of despair. She sat quietly and radiated empathy towards this new acquaintance.

Rose continued, "Thank you for being a friend to my mother; God knows she didn't have many. Her few friends and relatives either left or died, and she is isolated.

"When my brother left for California after dropping out of college, Mom really went downhill. While she never really came out and said it, he was clearly her favorite."

Cynthia could sense that the conversation was drifting towards a darker place. Rose's face seemed to lose color, and an unmistakable look of sadness appeared.

"You see, she gave most of her attention to him. The better presents, more attention, and most important, more love. No matter what I said, what I did, I rarely elicited a reaction from her. I could have run off and died and she probably wouldn't even have noticed."

Cynthia started to open her mouth in protest, but Rose put her hand up. "No, I am not mistaken! It was as obvious as the tail on Molly!

"John, on the other hand, could do no wrong. He never really did well in school, he hung out with the wrong crowd, got into drugs, and in short, was a total screw up.

"Still, my mother's face lit up every time he walked into the house. She would chide him for his misdeeds, but it always ended with a warm, motherly kiss. If he had died, I'm sure she would have jumped in the hole with him!

"One day after John and I came home with our report cards, I finally confronted my mother. You see, John came back with C's and D's and very unflattering comments about his efforts. I came back with A's and B's.

"He got a warm hug for passing his courses and I got a curt pat on the head. At dinner we only talked about him and his day.

"Later that night when John went to his room, I couldn't hold it back. I rehashed my childhood, searching for a reason for Mom's lack of love towards me. Finding no apparent reason, I started crying uncontrollably in front of my mother.

"'Rose, why are you crying? You did so well on your report card; what's up?'

"I managed to get out between tears, 'Why does John get all the attention? What have I done wrong? Am I too ugly? Why don't you love me?'

"My mother just stood there with her mouth wide open. For the longest time, nothing came out, but the color drained from her face. Eventually she uttered in a weak voice, 'Why do you say that?'

"'I love you just as much as I love John. You are my treasure. If it seems like I pay more attention to him it's because he needs more help.'

"She continued, 'Without pushing and prodding, he would be too lazy and give up. I know his weaknesses very well. In my younger days I have seen many men give into despair and become hobos, drunkards, and lost souls.

"'You, on the other hand, are like Aunt Sissy: smart, driven, and independent. Fortunately, you don't have Sissy's mean streak and short temper. I don't worry about you in the least.'

"'I'm sorry if I don't make you feel appreciated or pay you enough attention! I just didn't realize that I was neglecting you as I concentrated on getting John through life.'

"'Oh, I turned out to be a terrible mother, just as my own mother. Please forgive me and I will try to make it up to you. I love you as much as any person in the world.'

"My mom stopped talking and lifted my chin so that I was looking her right in the eyes. I shook my head in affirmation but in my heart, I knew it wasn't the truth! Her voice said one thing, but her eyes and heart showed another."

Rose stared at Cynthia and said in an assertive voice, "Girls are more in tune with their hearts, and while her words were registered, I knew she was lying.

"I dropped the confrontation and went to my bedroom. As I closed the door, I turned around and saw my mother covering her face with her head down."

Cynthia put her hands to her face and then patted Rose's hands. "Oh, I'm sure it was just your imagination. From the little I know of your mother, I find it hard to imagine she would act that way. She is so friendly to my dog and me, who until a few weeks ago, were complete strangers. Why would she be mean to you?"

"Oh, she was never overtly mean to me. I could have lived with that. If she yelled and screamed at me, I could have lived with that.

"It was the lack of attention and love. I felt like we lived on an island with a narrow bridge. John and Mom were on one side and I on the other.

"She would provide me with proper food and clothing and ask me about my day, but I felt like she was just doing a job. I never sensed true love and caring. Her face never lit up for me, but for John she beamed. Sometimes I thought I was a ghost daughter. I never completely understood why it was so.

"Even Aunt Sissy, whom I was close with, would acknowledge that it appeared so. When I asked her if it was something I did, she would just shrug her shoulders. I suspected she knew more than she let on, but I couldn't elicit an honest answer. She would just reply, 'It was nothing that you did; it just is.'

"Obviously, I blamed myself, and my self-esteem still suffers. If a mother can't love a child, maybe that child doesn't deserve to be loved.

"My shrink couldn't explain my mother's overwhelming favoritism. She surmised there is something in her past which guides her actions. She constantly reinforces that parents act out from their own upbringing, and their future unborn children suffer the consequences. The human mind is very formative from childhood experiences, and many innocent offspring suffer the consequences. She encourages me to build up my low self-esteem from within and not be brought down by outside influences."

Rose stopped talking, covered her face, and started crying. Cynthia patted her on the shoulders and said, "I'm sure your mother loves you very much."

After a few minutes Rose's sobs diminished and she replied, "Not really, and after fifty years I finally found out the truth!"

Rose bolted up, tears rolling down her face, and hurriedly walked away.

Cynthia's eyes popped open as her startled brain tried to process this unexpected revelation.

CHAPTER TWENTY

As Cynthia surmised, Rose was sitting on the same bench the very next day. Like her mother, she had a routine and a lot on her plate.

Cynthia sat down next to her as a sudden gust of wind swirled the browning leaves. Rose let a small smile appear and apologized to Cynthia. "I'm sorry about yesterday. I had no right to burden you with my problems. I barely know you, and there I was pouring my heart out. You must think I'm a train wreck. Anyway, how are you?"

"Oh, I'm fine Rose. You don't have to apologize for anything! I'm glad you went out of your way to let me know about your mother. How is she doing?"

"About the same. She is weak but that sharp mind and wit is still there. Just yesterday when I came back from seeing you, she noticed I had been crying. Did you know what that woman said?" Without waiting for an answer, Rose tried to imitate Esther's voice. "'What the hell are you crying for? I'm the one that's dying!'"

Cynthia couldn't help but let out a small chuckle as Rose continued.

"All the Shapiro sisters kept their mind, memories, and bitterness to the end.

"I remember when my Aunt Sissy was in a nursing home, she was a troublemaker. She would yell at all the nurses and constantly get into fights with the other patients. Her last words were to a nurse whom she didn't particularly like. 'I only wish you would die before me!'

"I don't know if it is genetics, upbringing, or circumstances but the Shapiro sisters were something else. Even Aunt Judy's two adult children don't speak to each other."

Cynthia could only respond, "Oh, come on, your mother is very nice. I'm sure they weren't much worse than other families."

"You couldn't be more wrong, my dear. Oh, the stories I could tell you! You really don't know the Shapiro sisters very well.

"My mother and deceased aunts held many a grudge from their childhood. Every little incident, bad argument, and betrayals are ingrained in their memory and influenced their lives. Whenever they got together, they relived past incidents that didn't go well. Even people that reminded them of old enemies were looked down upon.

"Once when we went to Coney Island with mom and Sissy, they stopped at a certain spot on the boardwalk. They had been contentedly chatting about the nice weather until they came to a certain spot marked by a ramp to the beach.

"Suddenly Sissy's demeanor changed. In her mean voice she yelled, 'This is the exact spot where that whore Betty Schultz stole my boyfriend, Morris!'

"She spit in the direction of the stairs. My mother countered, 'Oh, he wasn't your boyfriend; you went out a few times and he dumped you!'

"'No, no, no! Things were going great until *she* showed up in that floozy two piece bathing suit, strutting her tight butt and big boobs. I saw that look in his face; he couldn't take his eyes off her. He spent more time with her on that date than with me. He never called me again.

"'Well, at least I found out what kind of character Morris really was. He probably got lucky with that whore. I'm sure her butt has dropped, and her boobs have huge stretch marks. I hope they both rot in hell!'"

Cynthia put her hand to her mouth at the foul language. Who would think that old people would talk like that?

Rose cracked a smile at the surprised look on Cynthia's face. She continued. "Oh, there were many incidents like that. The Shapiro women had a reputation for those types of episodes.

"Perhaps the biggest blow up was when Judy came from upstate for a week's visit. Boring Uncle Ray decided he would let the sisters talk while he went for a drive. Not learning a lesson from the blowup the last time, the sisters quickly got into it!

"After the small talk of greetings and how big John and I had gotten, Sissy started the action. 'Well I hope you are happy upstate in a nice big house away from us peasants. I still can't get over how you abandoned us during the Depression!'

"Judy retorted, 'What the hell are you talking about? Ray is my husband; we are in love and moved to a nice area. What's your problem?'

"'Oh, bullshit, Judy. He was an opportunity! You got away from being poor, caring for a sick mother, and the responsibilities of running a household.'

"Judy, aghast, slapped Sissy so hard you would have thought it was thundering. Upon recovering, Sissy slapped back and let out a blood-curdling scream.

"Years of pent-up frustration and jealousy came rushing out. 'You left me here to take care of a sick mother, depressed father, and young Esther all by myself. I will never forgive you!'

"Judy, shocked at the suppressed truth being revealed, grabbed a handful of Sissy's hair. Sissy did likewise. They were locked in this physical battle like conjoined twins as the verbal war continued.

"Judy called Sissy an ugly, overweight spinster. 'You are just jealous because I am pretty and married, and you were stuck at home. Perhaps if you would lose weight, put on some makeup, and act like a lady, you could find a new husband.'

"Sissy spit in Judy's face and retorted, 'You really aren't that pretty. If you didn't spend hours fixing your hair, putting on makeup, and flirting like a five-dollar whore, you'd be unmarried too. Other than having some money, your husband is no great catch. You probably lead a life of complete boredom. I'd bet that you sleep in separate beds, fall asleep as Ray is talking, and can't wait for him to go to work. I'd wager sex with him is a nightmare and you can't wait for it to end. I'd rather slave away here than have that man on top of me. You'll probably pop out a few kids and raise dumb, ugly, boring children.'

"The wrestling match and insults continued until my mother, the youngest, threw a glass of water on them. Judy and Sissy let go of each other's hair and focused their anger on my mom."

"Before the aunts could act, Mom continued. 'Just stop the fighting; remember what happened the last time? I don't want to go to the emergency room again.' She yelled at them to shut up and forget the past, even as she couldn't.

"Judy yelled at my mother, 'Shut the hell up, you little twerp. Sissy is just a mean spinster and will always hate me.

ONE HUNDRED YEARS WITHOUT LOVE

Even though she is ugly, if she was nicer and perhaps put out a little, she could get married. Marriage doesn't have to be about true love. It can be a convenience to lead a better life. Forget the fairy tales! Pay attention, little sis; do you want to end up like bitter Sissy or satisfied pretty Judy?

"'I don't need this shit. I am happy upstate, and I thought it would be nice to see my city sisters. I guess I was wrong about that! You girls are too dumb to seize the right opportunities. I'm going back to my happy life away from this family.'

"She ran into the guest room, gathered her stuff, and waited outside. Ray eventually returned, and after a few minutes of arguing he threw his arms up. She threw her suitcase in the trunk, jumped in the passenger seat, slammed the car door, and took off. We didn't see or hear from Judy for years."

"Wow," Cynthia replied. "It sounds like your mom's family dynamics were crazy. Are your aunts still around?"

"Oh, they passed many years ago. I'd bet they are somewhere up there, still pulling each other's hair, cursing, and spitting. The Shapiro sisters never let anything go!"

Cynthia let out a small giggle as Rose continued. "My mother is just as bad as her older sisters. Everything is about the past and only the bad. You just haven't seen her enough to witness the anger built up inside."

Cynthia nodded her head in agreement, remembering the cursing Esther gave to the non-poop-picking-up jogger. When was the last time she had seen a centenarian give the middle finger?

Cynthia asked if she could visit Esther, but Rose just shook her head. "Mom really doesn't want any visitors right now. As a matter of fact, she told John and me to stay away; she doesn't want anybody to see her like this.

"I took the first flight from Chicago. I haven't seen my mom in five years, and we have a bad past. I wanted to make amends in case this was it. Things shouldn't go to the graveyard unresolved."

"Oh, I'm so sorry. I didn't realize things were that bad between you."

She sadly nodded her head in the affirmative and said, "Well, there was a big blow up many years ago; we both erupted. She finally insinuated that she never loved me like John."

"Oh, I'm sure you are just imagining it; sibling rivalry is very common."

"Oh, no, this is true! Mom finally came out and admitted it, and the reason why!"

Cynthia got very quiet and uncomfortable.

Rose sobbed and in a sorrowful voice said, "Well, at least she finally admitted what I sensed all along. The worst thing about it is that she hated me from the moment I was born!"

CHAPTER TWENTY-ONE

Cynthia's head snapped back as she processed those words. *She hated me from the moment I was born!* Her face turned pale, and she felt a sharp pain in her chest. Her mind clouded up in disbelief.

Did I hear things correctly? How could a mother dislike her own child at birth? Or for that matter, anytime? Even if my future children committed murder, I could never hate them. A mother conceived them, passed on her genes, nourished them from within, protected and loved them. She delivered and produced milk for them. No, no, no. Rose is mistaken. It is not possible!

Regaining her composure, Cynthia focused and said to the tearful Rose, "I'm sure you are mistaken that your mother doesn't love you. In fact, I'd bet she loves you very much. Sometimes our childhood memories are distorted and slights can be imagined. The human mind can play tricks, and misunderstandings happen all the time. I really think you are blowing things out of proportion."

"You can stop right there, Cynthia. I know you are friendly with my mother, and she likes you very much. But she is not the saint that you think she is.

"As I told you before, the Shapiro sisters were nasty, high-strung women. Perhaps it was their upbringing, the troubled times they lived through, or perhaps just pure genetics. They don't follow the basic concepts of love, children, and decency that you undoubtfully do.

"My earliest memories were of my father holding me, feeding and playing with me while mom would dote and spend more time with John. She was a great mom to John; I was just a drag to her. I remember catching frowns and harsh words when she attended to me.

"As a preschooler, I learned to avoid her when possible as I could sense her dislike of me. It's hard to like your mother when she dislikes you. I couldn't wait for John to come home from school. He was very nice and protective of me. He would take my hand, hug me, play with me, and provide some basic love. Dad also loved me. Unfortunately, he was away too much at work and played golf on Sundays.

"At the dinner table, the conversation was always about work, gossip, and John. My name rarely came up. In certain respects, I was like a ghost to my mother."

While taking in the information, Cynthia was involuntarily shaking her head. Rose, catching the gesture, stopped and confronted Cynthia. "Why are you doing that?"

Surprised by the confrontation, Cynthia replied, "You were only a young child. Many people perceive things that are simply aren't true or exaggerated. I'm sure there are parents that display favoritism, which may in fact be John in your case. Despite that, I'm sure your mother still loved you!"

"You are a very smart and intuitive girl, Cynthia; but in my case, I have proof that Mom hated me!"

Cynthia was about to argue, but Rose put her hand out in a stop signal. "Please, let me continue. I have never told a soul what I am about to tell you, because it hurts too much.

ONE HUNDRED YEARS WITHOUT LOVE

"In fact, sometimes I pretend that night was just a dream and didn't really occur. Yet, the truth is the truth, and it was real! One night when I was about six, I heard my parents arguing. I was in my bedroom asleep when I was awoken by my father's raised voice. 'Enough is enough, Esther! You had no reason to yell at Rose for not drying the dishes fast enough. My God, she is only six years old! Why do you always pick on her? It is obvious to everyone that you don't really like her. You never hug her, play with her, or for that matter even notice her. Yet for John you do anything and everything. Ever since she was born you have acted distant and downright nasty to her. I have seen the looks of annoyance from you when she tries to get attention. I have held my tongue up until now. I was hoping I was wrong and that things would get better, but they are not! I've tried to compensate for your shortcomings by showing her extra love and attention. I simply am not around enough to be both a good father and mother!

"'I have had enough of this nonsense; she is clearly suffering from some emotional issues. She is becoming withdrawn and appears depressed all the time. She doesn't play with the other kids anymore. She isn't washing her face, brushing her teeth, or trying to look decent. Her teacher says she is inattentive and daydreams during class. I'd say that poor motherhood is her problem. Goddamn it, Esther! What is the problem?'

"My mother started to scream back. 'What the hell are you talking about, Len? I treat my kids equal. How dare you accuse me of neglect when you are away most of the time!

"'I do the best I can with Rose. She is, in fact, a difficult child. As a baby she was colicky and kept us up constantly. She was always in trouble as a toddler, and I never had any peace. She has a short temper and cries at the slightest incident. In fact, sometimes she cries for no reason at all!

"'She is always dirty and has dark circles under her eyes. She has knots in her hair and always appears messy. She is not really the girl that I would have dreamed of having.'

"'Ah-ha, so you admit it. She is your child, God damn it! I don't care how she acts or looks. She is our child! We created her! She spent nine months inside of you! Your child's love should be unconditional! Esther, you are a decent woman with good morals. I know you had a rough childhood, and your mother and sisters are nuts. I bet that has something to do with your attitude towards Rose. God damn it, Esther, what is this all about?'

"There was quiet for a few moments, which I knew was trouble. I expected a quick denial, and maybe it was all in my head. I strained with all my might to hear my mother's response. With fear in my heart and a cold chill in my body, I waited for the truth.

"After perhaps one minute of absolute silence, I heard my mother sobbing. 'Oh, Len. I'm sorry. I had no idea it was so obvious. I have tried for years to overcome this lack of feeling for Rose. Yeah, you're right; I don't feel an attraction toward her. In fact, I actually feel revulsion in her presence. Please forgive me. Please. Please, please never tell her or for that matter another soul. I'll try to do better. I never realized it was that noticeable, or for that matter, affecting her that much. She doesn't deserve it. She is a nice girl but, but I still have a hard time loving her.'

"My father started shaking my mother. 'If you knew this all along, why didn't you tell me? We could have worked it out. We could have gotten you some counseling. Damn it! We could have made it better for Rose. I just hope it's not too late. We can still make it better! Do you even know why you have these feelings? She is a normal kid. She loves us unconditionally. I don't get it.'

"My mother, through tears and sobs, choked out, 'When I found out I was pregnant I initially loved the baby inside. When I felt her kicking, I couldn't wait to birth her, hold her, and love her. During that horrible, unbearable delivery, I still loved my baby.

"'After she was born, I passed out from the effort. The nurse awakened me and asked if I would like to hold my new baby girl. I slowly came to my senses and through the haze I remembered where I was. With love in my heart and the anticipation of seeing this child who lived inside of me, I held out my arms.

"'Of course I wanted to hold her. The nurse put the bundled up infant my arms and smiled.

"'She uncovered the baby's face, and I got my first look at Rose. That was the moment my love for her ended!'

"There was quiet for what seemed an eternity. I got up from my bed and walked toward the door to hear better. What did mama say?

"My six-year-old heart was beating rapidly, and I broke into a sweat. Then came the words that have altered my entire life.

"Esther, in a low and depressed voice said, 'My newborn baby girl looked exactly like my own mother, Jenny Shapiro!'

"My father, in disbelief, responded, 'So, I knew your mother; she wasn't the nicest human being that ever lived, but that is no reason for hate. For God's sake, she was your mother!'

"He paused and let the last statement sink in. Esther put her head down in shame and didn't respond.

"After a few moments, my father continued his barrage. 'Moreover, whatever happened between you and your mother is over. Use some common sense. The past is behind us; you must think about your daughter's future.'

"Still my mother didn't lift her head or respond. She started shaking and crying uncontrollably. I heard her fall to the floor, and I creaked the door open slightly.

"My mother was hunched up in a ball, crying hysterically. My father likewise got on his knees and started shaking my mother. 'Esther, snap out of it! We all have childhood traumas. You are stronger than letting your past destroy this family! Get over it. For God's sake and the sake of our daughter, get over it!'

"My mother finally looked up and stared past my father's face. She seemed to be looking towards a far-off area. As it turns out, it was a far-off time!

"'You don't understand Len. You couldn't possibly understand. It was not how my mother treated me. It is about how she destroyed my father. For that I can never forget or forgive!'"

CHAPTER TWENTY-TWO

"Not being loved at home, I became rebellious. I was born in 1953, two years after John. By the time I was about twelve, it was the 1960's and America was changing. The Vietnam War was escalating and making the regular news. There were race riots in several major cities. Civil unrest was the norm!

"The Beatles debuted on the Ed Sullivan Show in February of 1964 and the wild sixties took off. They called us the revolutionary generation.

"Soon people were growing long hair, dressing in ripped clothes, and not wearing bras. Protesters against the escalating war were staging sit-ins at colleges. When a mandatory draft was created to send our young men into a foreign war, there were countless rebellions. Kids started burning draft cards and some draftees fled to Canada.

"The cultural shift took off from there. The younger generation decided they could no longer conform to antiquated conventional life. Young people decided that happiness, not material things, was the key to life.

"These self-proclaimed hippies decided that love and peace, not hate and war, were their future. They experimented with drugs, not as a way of getting high, but as a way to see reality differently. They saw nature colorfully and saw the

Earth and themselves as one. Sex became a normal expression of freedom and a normal biological urge. The advent of birth control pills helped allow this freedom.

"Not really satisfied with my life at home and feeling lonely, I started hanging out with kids that followed the hippie movement. They preached love and peace and welcomed all. We left conventional thinking and prejudices behind.

"We hung out after school and smoked weed. While I was nervous at first with these strange kids, the unconditional friendship, love, and companionship fulfilled my needs.

"I started cutting class, and my grades began slipping. You'd think my mother would have been upset and confrontational, but her reactions were remarkably mild. She would, however, criticize me for looking unkempt and wearing torn clothes.

"After a few minor scoldings with little effect, she eventually threw her arms up and said, 'Oh, the hell with you. Do as you want.'

"I was still rebellious, but it didn't eliminate the hurt I felt knowing my mom wouldn't try harder. My shrink suggested that I turned to rebellion to get more motherly attention. Thinking back on it, the shrink was probably right!"

Cynthia was transfixed as she didn't know much about the Vietnam War or the hippie movement of the sixties. She thought to herself, *Here is a witness to history and I get to hear it.*

Rose smiled. "You know, those times were very special. We developed a spiritual awakening, unlike our parents.

"The older generation was very materialistic at that time. Cars, televisions, and new appliances were very important to them. They bought into the communist takeover of the world propaganda and largely supported the war. They bought into President Johnson's lies about America's military actions.

"The facts came out later that accidental bombings of civilian villages killed more South Vietnamese than communist soldiers. Poverty, death, and starvation of the innocents were kept secret.

"To us, love, peace, openness, and tolerance were more important than things. We protested the war and Washington's lies. We experimented with LSD and marijuana to heighten our senses. We were more open about sex in those days, and I was fortunate not to get pregnant or catch a venereal disease. We hung out in friends' houses, drank, smoked pot, and listened to rock and roll. Janis Joplin, Santana, The Grateful Dead, Jefferson Star Ship, and Jimi Hendrix… oh, they were the best!"

Cynthia sat quietly and somewhat in shock over this woman's revelations. She was trying to imagine this seventy-year-old woman as a young girl. Even more bizarre was imagining her as a longhaired, braless, promiscuous, spiritual hippy.

"The best weekend of my entire life was Woodstock 1969."

CHAPTER TWENTY-THREE

She turned around to Cynthia with an incredulous gleam in her eyes and a huge smile on her face. To Cynthia's surprise, Rose's wrinkles became less pronounced, her skin took on a glow, and her voice grew younger. Those old grey pupils seemed to lighten and dilate. The wind kicked up, and some leaves ascended and reattached to the tree.

"Have you ever heard of Woodstock?"

Cynthia, startled by Rose's apparent metamorphosis and the sudden gust of wind, was speechless. She thought to herself, Am I dreaming or did time just regress?

After a few moments she responded, "Well, I have heard of it, but to be honest I don't know much about it. No offense, but as far as I recall it was a about a bunch of hippies doing drugs, having sex, rolling around in mud, and listening to rock and roll music."

Rose just laughed. "No offense taken, my dear. The history books and older generation put it out that way. They couldn't possibly understand it!

"Woodstock was arguably the pivotal event in a revolution against conventionalism. It was the probably the largest non-violent, peaceful event in the history of the world. It changed about a half million people's lives' forever!

ONE HUNDRED YEARS WITHOUT LOVE

"It was about awakening, a freeing of the spirit, being in tune with nature. The sixties were really a turbulent time. Besides the Vietnam War and the race riots, there were the assassinations of the Kennedy brothers and Martin Luther King, Jr. We had the Cold War and were under threat of a nuclear attack from Russia. Drugs and birth control pills were readily available, and believe me, were eagerly used.

"We got away from the war, the protests, the nagging parents, the pressures of school and conforming to the older generation. It was a very misunderstood concert. It didn't start out to be this huge historical event which shook the world. It was supposed to be a simple concert for about 50,000 people.

"As a matter of fact, I didn't even plan on going. Tickets were too expensive, and I wasn't that interested. I was sitting at home that Friday of the concert in 1969 when my cousin, Allison, called.

"She was at the concert and was screaming for me to join her. She said it was amazing and that I ought to get myself over there. She insisted that it was only two hours away and it was an event not to be missed.

"I told her I'd love to, but I had no money for tickets and no ride to get there. She insisted that there were so many people that security was overrun, and people weren't paying to get in.

"'Yeah, but I have no place to stay and don't have a suitcase to pack things.'

"'Don't bring things; bring yourself! We are sleeping in the fields and being with nature. The music is amazing, everybody is high, and it is the ultimate blast! Find someone with a car and get yourself over here.' The phone clicked, and I stood in confusion and conflict.

"At that point in my life, I was torn between two worlds. Meat was the foundation of a healthy diet; The Sound of

Music was the popular movie. Men and women wore suits and dresses to work. The world was boring and in danger of a nuclear war. I was still a conservative, law-abiding teenager who was a decent student. At that time, I had aspirations of college, marriage, maybe a few kids and enjoy a nice quiet existence."

"Yet, in spite of my basic needs being met and wishes for a good future I was an unhappy, unfulfilled teenager. I had a few girlfriends, no boyfriend, and felt unloved by my own mother. I was neither a raving beauty nor a genius and was socially awkward. While I existed, there was an empty feeling inside. I learned later from my shrink; it was called clinical depression.

"At that moment I made a decision that would change me forever. I needed to break the bonds of my empty life and try something else.

"I convinced my friend, Carly, to drive and we set out the following morning. We didn't have tickets for the event, but we set out anyway. My mother asked where I was going since I was carrying a bag full of clothes.

"'I'm going away with Carly; I'll be back Monday!'

"I walked out without waiting for a response. As expected, but still hurtful, she made no attempt to stop me.

"It started raining on the way upstate, and Carly suggested we turn around. '"We don't have tickets, we don't have a hotel, and we don't have money; what the hell are we thinking?'

"Empowered by my mother's apathy, I raised my voice. 'We have ourselves.

"'Besides, my cousin is there, and she said it's a blast. Kids are sleeping in the fields, eating granola, doing drugs, and listening to rock 'n' roll! The establishment isn't there, and we can get away from our boring lives. This will be awesome! Maybe we can meet some cute guys.'

ONE HUNDRED YEARS WITHOUT LOVE

"Carly's eyes lit up, she thrust her arm forward, and floored the gas pedal. 'Cute guys here we come!'

"As we got nearer to Bethel, where the concert was being held, traffic came to a halt. We looked for miles around and it was total chaos. Not only were cars stationary, but also hippie kids were sitting on car roofs, half naked, smoking marijuana.

"Some frustrated kids pushed their cars off the road and started walking towards the festival. We asked how far away it was, and the best answers were about ten miles.

"They just smiled and said, 'Everybody in the freakin' world is going.' Carly and I looked at each other, and since we were locked in traffic anyway, we pulled off to the side and joined the caravan.

"The long trek to the festival was an experience I'll never forget. Boys and girls we'd never met before wrapped their arms around us and were so friendly. They asked our names, where we were from, and if we hated the materialistic world like themselves. They passed around joints, and we smoked and drank together.

"One guy had the longest hair I'd ever seen and played guitar as we walked. The songs were about love and peace and higher awakenings. I don't know if it was the drugs, atmosphere, or rebellious talk, but I felt in a higher state of consciousness.

"Colors became more vibrant, the trees seemed alive, and the sky seemed to be bluer and embracing; I was in tune with the entire universe. I could even sense what the animals were thinking and doing. We were all as one.

"I felt weightless, and my blood was coursing effortlessly through my body. The worries of my life lightened as I felt loved by everybody and everything.

"Carly hooked up with a scraggly looking guy and they walked with the guy's arm around her neck. He would occasionally grope her butt, and she would laughingly push his hand away. She really didn't mind!

"The ten-mile walk was a festival by itself. I was truly transfixed by the young, disheveled group of people. They acted as if they didn't have a care in the world, or for that matter care anything about the outside world. Nobody looked down on anybody else. I'd never felt love, kinship, and freedom like that before!

"Eventually we reached a huge open field with a stage and scaffolding and, like, a million kids listening to Santana. Girls were sitting on boys' shoulders, moving to the beat with starry eyes and just a little bit of clothing. Most of the guys were shirtless and filthy with mud. It was a rain-soaked event with little shelter, but nobody seemed to care.

"The few food vendors there had quickly run out of hotdogs and hamburgers, and some workers handed out drug-laced granola. This added fuel to the fire of this event.

"The few latrines present began to overflow, and poop and pee began flowing towards the crowd. While it sounds disgusting, nobody seemed to mind. There was a small lake near the event, and people bathed stark naked in it."

Cynthia put her hands to her face in revulsion, but Rose just laughed. "Oh, for God's sake, don't be so shocked!

"Those were different times; America was a turbulent place. Any day we could have been nuked, sent off to war, or killed in a race riot. The older generation was hooked on materialism and didn't care about human suffering. Husbands often cheated on their wives as they sat home, raised kids, and baked pies. We were a counterculture. We showed open love and care for the world. We brought in a new age of rock 'n' roll music. Some people say we changed the world!"

CHAPTER TWENTY-FOUR

"Anyway, we managed to squeeze in between a group of hippies, and they welcomed us with hugs and kisses. 'Welcome to nirvana,' one of them said. Carly and her new friend, Rick, started necking and I turned away. While Carly was a good friend, I did not always approve of her loose lifestyle.

"While this place was enlightening, I was still a conservative girl with an inferiority complex at heart. *Who would want me?* I thought to myself. *I'll probably be by myself in short order.*

"As I turned away from Carly and Rick, I noticed a cute guy staring in disgust at Carly and Rick going at it. As he fixated on them, I fixated on him. There was something about this stranger that enthralled me.

"He seemed totally out of place in this environment. He was wearing jeans and a casual blue shirt, which was clean and nice fitting. His hair was short and blond; he was clean-shaven, and his demeanor was different. He didn't appear high or entranced by the atmosphere. As a matter of fact, he seemed uncomfortable – and maybe even disgusted – by the behaviors of the crowd.

"While never a beauty in my younger days, my skin was clear, my hair long and straight, and I had a nice figure. His eyes eventually strayed from Carly and Rick and traveled in my direction. Our eyes met and locked.

"After a few seconds of direct stare, he slid over towards me. My heart started racing, butterflies fluttered in my stomach, and my mind was in a whirlwind. *Oh, my God,* I thought to myself, *is this really happening?*

"He got within a foot and shyly introduced himself. His name was Jimmy, he was twenty-one, and was with some friends. I stammered out my name, lied about my age, and pointed out Carly. He laughed and said, 'Well, she appears to be having a good time.' He politely asked if I minded him coming over and being near me. I nodded and let out a nervous giggle, and we started talking.

"Quill was playing, and it was getting hard to hear each other. We stopped trying to converse and just sat back. It was somewhat strange being near each without talking, yet it seemed comfortable.

"I had never had a boyfriend before and was unsure how to act. Carly and her new friend were kissing passionately near us, and it was awkward. Luckily, the lead singer from the band helped us out.

"During the song 'Stone Believer,' he started throwing small blocks of wood into the audience and Jimmy reached up and grabbed one. Looking at the block and then staring at me, he placed the block in my open hand and smiled at me. My eyes locked on his pale blue eyes and this showing of generosity.

"Though he was a stranger, I sensed a connection which I'd never felt before. He slowly inched his hand towards mine, and I didn't move away. His touch was tender, smooth, and warm. I turned my head away for a moment and felt a warm sensation encasing my entire body.

"As the music continued and the audience was swaying, he got closer. Soon our bodies were touching, and we started swaying to the music. My nervousness eased, my body relaxed, and my mind blended with Jimmy's. We were in unison! *Is this what love feels like?* I asked myself.

"Between songs we held hands and talked as if we were old friends. He had graduated from college and was working as a junior accountant in Manhattan. Surprised, I asked him what the hell an accountant was doing at a hippie rock concert. Jimmy just smiled and said, 'You and me both! My crazy friends literally came over my house and yanked me out of bed. That is my friend, Rick, over there exploring your friend's tongue. They said we were going on a road trip, and I was coming along. I initially protested but my mother intervened and encouraged me to go and have some fun. She thought a twenty-one-year-old kid shouldn't be sitting at a desk all day.

"'I don't think she really knew what kind of event this would be. For that matter, I couldn't have imagined this either. There must be, like, a million people here!

'I really regretted coming here until just now. These are not my type of people, and I feel out of place. People are handing out drug laced Kool-Aid, and there is no food. The line to the latrines is crazy long, and shit is literally oozing out.

'Guys aren't wearing shirts, and girls are showing way too much skin for my taste. Some people are bathing naked in a lake nearby. There are groups of kids on the outskirts having sex in broad daylight.'

"I shook my head in agreement as he continued. 'We had to sleep in this field last night and it started raining. This is not what a nice German boy from Queens is used to. Luckily, it was hot as hell and we dried off quickly. My friends tried to get me to smoke some marijuana, which I politely refused. While the music isn't bad, this is just not my thing. I was plotting an early escape until a little while ago.'

"Not turned off by his admissions, I asked apprehensively, 'Why did you change your mind about leaving?' I looked downward in case his answer wasn't the one I wanted to hear. After seventeen years of love deprivation, the hurt would be hard to bear.

"'Well,' he answered, 'I just met a girl I can't take my eyes off of. She has long straight hair and a lovely smile. She looks innocent and pure, and her eyes are large and inviting. I'm a little afraid I could get lost in them if I stare too long.'

"I was afraid to look up, but my heart raced, my skin tingled, and I was very nervous. Was he talking about me?

"Jimmy continued, 'Her voice is soft but firm. I really don't know much about her, but I'd love to find out more. If she wants to hang out with me, I could be persuaded to stay!'

"I was too nervous to ask who this person was, but my heart was pounding in anticipation. I looked up into his eyes, and neither of us spoke. The world suddenly got silent except for my pounding heartbeat. I felt like Jimmy and I were alone in a small room.

"He slowly moved closer, and I froze. He got inches from my face and just stared at me. Never having had a boyfriend before, I was nervous as hell. I always had the feeling that nobody would be interested in me. I always imagined that I was not deserving of love.

"Suddenly his lips touched mine, and my heart rate settled down. I returned his kiss, and we embraced and started making out."

Rose turned towards Cynthia to see her reaction. Cynthia put her hands to her mouth and muttered, "Wow, what a story. Please continue."

ONE HUNDRED YEARS WITHOUT LOVE

Thrilled by Cynthia's encouragement, Rose started speaking again. "My whole body was tingling, and I felt like I was floating on air.

"The rest of the day we spent hand in hand and rocked to the music. By nightfall he had his shirt unbuttoned, had smoked a joint, and we walked around the outskirts of the crowd. As we walked by a lake, we heard splashing and talking. We parted the bushes, and there were young people, naked and romping around. Some were cleaning the mud off themselves, but others were kissing and making out. As we gazed further, we could see others on the outskirts engaged in sex."

Rose saw Cynthia put her hands to her mouth in shock. Cynthia said, "My God. They were really having sex outside in the middle of the day?"

Rose smiled. "I know it seems slutty and promiscuous, but during those three days it was natural, and people were uninhibited. Most people were dissociated from regular life, and their spirits were in a different place. We were the young generation ready to challenge a conservative, capitalistic, war-raging society.

"We were more connected to nature, divine purpose, and most importantly, peace and helping our fellow human beings. Everybody loved each other, with the exception of the perceived oppressive establishment. People were handing out food and blankets to others. If someone overdosed, they were taken to the medical tent. Girls sat on strange boys' shoulders to hear and cheer to the music. The drugs, the mud, the rain, the love was the most natural thing at that festival. More importantly for me, I had someone to love and make me feel good about myself.

"Jimmy and I went back to our little group, and during a break in the music I heard a small group playing a Joan Baez song from the previous night. The female vocalist sang low, but my ears immediately caught the words above the crowd's babble.

We shall overcome.
We shall overcome.
Deep in my heart I do believe we shall overcome someday.
We shall be alright.
We shall be alright.
Deep in my heart I do believe we shall be alright someday.

"Tears started flowing freely. I'm not sure why, but it was uncontrollable. A lifetime of guilt and poor self-esteem lifted, and my body and mind felt a new sense of purpose.

"Jimmy asked, 'What's the matter? Are you all right?' I just shook my head and tuned out everything but the song. As the girl's low voice preached hope and encouragement, I began to relax like I never had before.

"I experienced an out of body experience for the first and only time of my life. I looked up and the sky was the brightest blue I ever saw. Like an angel lifting from the ground, my sight seemed to rise from my body and view the whole grounds. Surrounded by 400,000 people, I was the center of everybody's attention. Boys, girls, band members, and security people were patting me and hugging me.

"They were praising my beauty, my accomplishments, and my character. I had never felt such joy and euphoria in my life. When the song stopped, I just hugged Jimmy and didn't let go for a long time. I'm sure everybody thought I was on LSD, but

ONE HUNDRED YEARS WITHOUT LOVE

I wasn't! I was high on the peace, love, and friendship of the festival.

"I'm sure Jimmy was bewildered by my actions, but he accepted me for how I acted and who I was. He enveloped me, and our bodies became as one. We fell asleep about midnight.

"As we slept, we heard songs from Creedence Clearwater Revival and Janis Joplin. As loud as the music was, I was near Jimmy and felt contentment. If this is what it felt like to be in love, I was all in! I thought I was in heaven.

"About 3:30 am, we were awakened by the crowd rising and cheering. Sly and The Family Stone just came on and got the crowd going, like nothing I'd ever imagined.

"It was pitch black, but nothing mattered. The microphones erupted with a spark that ignited a half million young kids. It was like people rising from the dead with unbridled energy. Everybody went crazy! Girls hopped on boys' shoulders, and everybody swayed to the music.

"Jimmy and I were marginal participants but when they played 'Dance to the Music' we got into it. The band's energy, the crowd's enthusiasm, and an unexplainable lifting of inhibitions all kicked in! My mind and body were out of control; the crowd moved as one and I loved it. It was an incredible event, and I was there!

"I didn't think they could top the excitement of that song, but they did. Two songs later they sang 'I want to take you higher.' Soon a cloud of marijuana pervaded our nostrils and the crowd became delirious."

Rose stopped and turned to Cynthia. She was radiating happiness at the memories of that historical event. Cynthia was trying to picture Rose as a wild-eyed young hippie girl. She had trouble blending in the past and present Rose!

Rose said, "I know it sounds like a wild drug party, but it was the best time of my life. I never felt hungry or tired or out of place. I felt love, peace, and total contentment for the first time in my life. Oh, how I wish for those days again!"

CHAPTER TWENTY-FIVE

That night, Cynthia's husband noticed her disengaged and in deep thought. He asked if everything was okay, but she didn't respond. He grabbed her by the shoulders, turned her around, and saw a bewildered look in her eyes.

"Steve," she asked inquisitively, "how can a mother not love a child?"

Steve stood bewildered for a few seconds and asked, "What the hell brought on that question?"

She noticed Steve get nervous, imagining some tragedy on the news. "Oh, it's not about me or any of our friends; it's about the old lady I have been meeting at the park. She is very sick, and her daughter flew in from Chicago.

"I've been talking to the daughter these last few days. She has had a troubled life and is unburdening herself. She says her mother hates her and always has."

"Phew," Steve replied as he let out a breath of relief. "I thought you were going to tell me you changed your mind about having kids. Remember, right after I complete my residency it will be baby making time!"

After a small smile, Cynthia continued. "Well, it does make you think when so many people relay a sad childhood. This woman, Rose, insists she is not imagining being unloved; she insists her mother told her directly. It seems so hard to believe.

"Her mother, Esther Shapiro, is the one-hundred-year-old woman that I have been seeing this past month. She is an interesting person who has lived a tough life. She certainly has some rough edges, says nasty things, rehashes some old bitter stories, and even tried to physically attack a woman in the park. Still, she is very kind to Molly and me, and I sense that she is basically a nice person. Could her troubled past have turned her into a bitter old lady? Could it have made her hate members of her own family? Could it even make her hate her very own daughter?

"I have heard horrible stories of parents killing their own children, but they were usually found to be insane. Steve, how can this be?"

Steve answered in his typical all-knowing manner. "You know in med school we rotated through the psych unit. We got mini tutorials by psychologists, psychiatrists, and social workers. I do recall a lecture on unloving parents; let me see if I can find my notes."

Cynthia stared into space as Steve went into his study. She heard drawers slamming and books being opened. Soon Steve came out with a spiral notepad. "Here, take a look!"

Cynthia moved over, put her arm around Steve, and listened. Steve started to read from his notes.

"Wow, this is interesting; it says that parental love is not a given. In fact, the problem is fairly common. They actually categorize six types of unloving parents.

"The first type are disturbed people, like sociopaths, alcoholics, and drug abusers. The second type is depressed people; they are incapable of love due to their own misery. The third type is the angry parent who yells and flies off the handle often. The fourth type is the narcissistic parent who sees their children as an extension of themselves and withholds love when the child underperforms. The fifth type is the controlling parent, and the last type are those that play favorites."

Cynthia's thoughts went from her usual boredom whenever Steve went medical to thoughtfulness when she heard that favoritism could be a factor. She thought to herself, *Rose insisted that her brother was Esther's favorite. Could the Shapiro sister's anger and jealousness flow over and doom Rose?* She tuned Steve out as he continued reading his notes.

That night, she dreamed of a future in which she had two children: an older daughter and a son two years younger. They were at a playground and Cynthia was holding the toddler son. He was cooing and had his arms wrapped around Cynthia, planting little kisses on her cheek. He had the bluest eyes, and his hair had curls with locks that pointed skyward. His complexion was milky white without a blemish. All the neighbors remarked what a beautiful child he was, just like his mother. She remembered what an easy pregnancy and delivery she'd had with this beautiful child. He kind of slid out and smiled immediately. She felt an instant lifelong bond to this child.

The sister, four years old, was playing on the swings with some friends. Her face was dirty, her hair disheveled, and she had a loud raspy voice. As Cynthia looked up at the large, rather unattractive girl, her thoughts flashed back to her first delivery, which in her dream was excruciating. In her dream, the girl was colicky and difficult as a toddler.

The daughter joined a group of girls on the raised play area, and her voice could be heard above all the others. As the mothers were engaged in their own conversation, suddenly a fight arose amongst the playing children. The girls were on the top platform, fighting about who would go down the slide next. The argument escalated into screaming, and soon, pushing. Before the mothers could intervene, Cynthia's daughter pushed another girl off the apparatus and the girl fell with a thud.

The girl's mother ran over to her daughter screaming, "Oh my God!" The child arose with a bloody nose and scrapes across her arms and legs. The mother scooped her up and turned to Cynthia.

"Your daughter is an undisciplined little devil! She constantly quarrels with the other kids, and now look what she's done! You are a bad parent and offer little discipline or guidance. Don't you ever let your child near mine again."

Before Cynthia could apologize, the other mothers nodded in agreement and took their children away.

Cynthia was overwhelmed and speechless. She gazed at the bleeding, hysterical child and all the other mothers' backs toward her.

Cynthia's daughter gazed at the scene from the top of the jungle gym. She climbed down the apparatus and nervously approached Cynthia.

Cynthia gazed into her child's dark brown eyes in silence. The child looked nervous and put her head down. 'I'm sorry, Mommy, but Emma clogged up the slide and wouldn't let anybody pass."

How could my daughter do this thing? Does she show remorse about the injured child? Will this type of behavior continue? Surely my baby boy wouldn't do such a thing.

The dream ended and she awoke in a state of despair.

CHAPTER TWENTY-SIX

Rose was sitting on the bench the next day. Her head was down, and she was crying into a handkerchief. She seemed in a faraway place and wasn't aware as Cynthia and Molly approached. Sensing something unpleasant was going on, Cynthia started to back away. She didn't want to disturb the obviously upset woman. Molly, wanting to see Rose, started barking and pulling towards the distressed woman.

The sudden jerking of the leash caused Cynthia to lose her grip and the excited Pomeranian ran to the bench. Jolted out of her trance, Rose gazed up and Molly triumphantly jumped into her arms.

"'Oh, hi, Cynthia. I didn't notice you approaching. It's nice to see you again; I was afraid my self-pity stories might have driven you away." She patted Molly, who planted several licks on her face.

"Oh, you are such a precious little thing. I wish I had one just like you. If only people loved unconditionally like dogs, the world would be in a better place."

She turned towards Cynthia and said, "Did you know that dog spelled backward is God?"

Without waiting for a reply, she flatly said, "Mom isn't doing too well. The antibiotics aren't working, and she seems a little weaker. The doctor is not optimistic that she will recover. Although she can barely talk, she still asks where John is.

"I keep telling her that he is in California with his family and his work. She then responds, 'Well, don't bother him with my illness then.'

"She obviously wants to see him and believes that she is dying but refuses to let me tell him. I'm wondering if I should do it anyway."

Putting her hand on her chin she said, "I'm not really sure what the right thing is. I probably should just call John and tell him to get himself over here pronto. This may be his last opportunity to see Mom alive.

"But, anytime in the past that I did something against Mom's wishes, terrible things followed. If I had a dollar for every time she threatened to disown and never speak to me again, I'd be a rich woman. John, on the other hand, could do anything and always come up smelling like roses."

Suddenly Rose stopped talking and turned pale. Beads of sweat appeared on her face, and she swayed to the left. Cynthia was able to catch her movement and righted the older woman.

"Oh, my Lord. I'm so sorry! Sometimes when I think of past fights with my mom, I get lightheaded. Usually it's not that bad."

Cynthia stroked her back, and Rose added, "It's like getting punched in the stomach repeatedly. I'm sure it's hard for you to comprehend, but after a life of being second fiddle, it can turn physical. My shrink used to insist that the mind has great control of the body.

"I used to develop these strange stomach pains, and when given medicines they became joint and muscle pains. I went to several doctors, and after continuous testing nothing was ever discovered. In my teens I developed debilitating migraines, which medicines didn't alleviate. Both a neurologist and psychiatrist hypothesized that were stress related."

Cynthia seemed a bit confused. "Why did you see a psychiatrist for headaches?"

"Well," Rose answered, "I was seeing a psychologist for depression and low self-esteem. I have been in counseling since I was sixteen and taking medicines for clinical depression. Through years of counseling, it appears the cause of my mental issues are due to a poor relationship with my mother.

"I have endured so much stress from encounters with her that my body is suffering the consequences. We had a major blowup about ten years ago. To survive, I had gotten away and relocated to Chicago. We barely acknowledged each other and just sent birthday cards. That is why I have stayed away for so long."

Cynthia put her hands to her mouth and gasped. "You haven't spoken to your mom in over ten years?"

Rose just nodded her head as tears rolled down her face. "Yeah, I know it sounds like I am a terrible daughter, but it was the only way I could survive!

"I have created a new life in Chicago, I have a decent job and have some friends. My physical ailments are better, but a day doesn't go by without pain in my heart."

As Rose paused, Cynthia couldn't help but ask, "If you don't mind talking about it, what was the cause of the blowup that sent you away? Did you two get into a physical fight or something? If you don't want to talk about it, I totally understand."

Rose just put her head down and became silent. Cynthia, sensing she'd stepped into upsetting territory, started to apologize for butting in. As she was apologizing, Rose put up her hand and blurted out, "It was set off over DOG POOP."

Cynthia stopped in her tracks and tried to grasp her meaning. "What did you say? Did you just say dog poop?"

Rose nodded her head, and in a lowered sad tone she said, "Yeah. Dog poop.

"Do you really want to hear the story? It is really crazy, and I have never told it to anyone before."

Really wanting to hear what sent Rose 800 miles away Cynthia coyly responded, "Only if it doesn't cause you too much pain."

"I have been in pain my whole life. That incident just ignited fifty years of resentment, hurt, and anger from an unloving mother.

"It was Mother's Day 2007. John was in California, and Jimmy was long gone. I was living in Queens and working for an accounting firm in Kew Gardens. While Mom and I weren't exactly on great terms, we talked once a week and I visited her every few months here in Floral Park.

"We were like two strangers every time we met, and conversations were awkward at best. We would discuss the weather and current news, but little about the past. Inevitably she would ask if I had spoken to John as she rarely heard from him.

"Well, this particular Mother's Day I took her to lunch at a fancy restaurant in town, and we had a reasonably good time. My heart was always heavy around her, as I knew she didn't really like me. Believe me, if she wasn't my mother I wouldn't have bothered with her.

"It was a nice day out for her. Several waiters and patrons acknowledged what a nice mother and daughter we made.

ONE HUNDRED YEARS WITHOUT LOVE

They congratulated Mom on having such a sweet daughter to take her out on this special day.

"After lunch, as we arrived near her house, she asked if we could sit for a while at this very park. It was a beautiful spring day and I had nothing else going on.

"As we sat on this very bench, she became very quiet and appeared downcast. 'Mom, what is it? We have just had a nice time, you got to go out, and it is a beautiful day. Why are you acting so sad?'

"Mom didn't respond but started to sob. I sat there, bewildered, but knew better than to push the issue. Her sobbing was interrupted by a group of boys laughing and running with a Golden Retriever. She watched the group cross in front of our bench with the dog by their side. A smile came to her face as the dog looked her way and barked as if to say hello."

"Suddenly the dog stopped, started to sniff the grass, and pooped under a tree a few yards away from us. The boy holding the dog searched his pockets for a bag to collect the waste.

"In despair he discovered his pockets were empty and asked if anybody else had a bag. The other boys just laughed and joked, 'Why would we be carrying a dog poop bag? We don't have a dog.'

"One of the boys raised his voice and said, 'John, forget the dog shit. Let's get to the rec center. The game starts in ten minutes.'

"The boy, John, whose dog did the poop unhappily nodded his head and the group took off. My mother was frozen when she heard the name John. Suddenly, she lurched backwards, her body shook and she turned ghostly white.

"I stared at my mom and asked if she was okay. She didn't respond, and I could sense her deep in thought. Slowly she lowered her head and said to no one in particular, 'So that's what you think of me.'

"I waited a few seconds to figure out what she meant. My thoughts were muddled, and I was bewildered over Mom's behavior. What just happened?

"A group of boys were running with a Golden Retriever, the dog pooped, and the kids ran to the rec center. What was I missing?

"As Mom sobbed in silence, I closed my eyes and replayed the episode over and over. As the images and voices replayed themselves, I finally picked up the missing pieces: John and uncollected dog poop.

"So that's what you think of me!

"I grabbed my mother by the shoulder and gently shook her back to the present. She raised her head and locked her eyes onto mine.

"'Why am I upset, you ask? How should I feel? Do you know what it's like to raise a son, treat him like royalty, love him with all your being, and then he barely acknowledges that you are even alive!'

"'John didn't send a Mother's Day card, give me a call, or even acknowledge that he has a mother. I haven't heard from him in years!

"'Why am I upset? God damn you, Rose! Use your common sense, if you even have any. Do you know what a mother goes through when her child ignores her? You have no idea.'

"I just sat there, paralyzed. I felt like I just got punched in the stomach. My body became numb, and I couldn't talk. I started shaking and became light-headed.

"What the hell, I thought. I spent all this time and effort helping my mother, and all she can think about is John. No thank you, no pat or hug in appreciation. I might as well have been an inanimate object for all the affection she showed me.

"My father was long dead, my brother three thousand miles away, my husband deceased, and my own mother couldn't care less. What did I do to deserve this? Was it me? Was I unworthy of love? Why did everything I touch turn to shit?

"My mind swam in chaos, and I felt that I was sinking in quicksand. As I got lightheaded and almost ready to pass out, I blurted, 'Mom what about me?' Pointing to myself I said, 'I am here, and I love you. We had a good time today. Enjoy the day and forget about John for the moment!'

"Before I could put my hand down, she swatted it aside. 'Forget my Johnny? What kind of mother do you think I am?'

"Her eyes became glossy and she stared into space. I grew nervous for a second as I thought she might be having a stroke. Had I pushed her too far?

"Staring at the cloudless sky but viewing the past, Esther continued. 'You know I grew up during the Depression. We had nothing during that time! I mean nothing! We never knew where our next meal was coming from. We lived in fear of being evicted from our home.

"'My only ray of light and reason to go on was the love of my father! He was the only one who paid attention to me, or for that matter cared that I was around. My sisters thought that I was a burden, and my mother treated my father likewise when he was out of work. We developed a bond of kindred spirits and kept ourselves going.

"'Whenever my mother berated my father, I came to his side and pulled him away. I tried to push my mother into the other room and told her to leave him alone. Her reaction was always calling us two peas in a pod. She created bad names for both of us: good for nothing and useless. I swore to make his life as happy as possible, and he did the same for me.

"'When my father died, I felt like jumping in after him. How was I going to live without him?'

"I sat there speechless as my mother went on. I realized that she was reliving the past in her childhood apartment.

"Esther continued, 'Eventually I married your father, but my heart was still unfulfilled. I didn't know why I still felt empty, yet I wasn't happy. What was the matter with me?

"'I went through the expected routine of a young married woman: cleaning, cooking, and making friends in the suburbs. From outside appearances, things were fine. Yet there was this hole inside my heart and a sense of something missing. I developed a recurring dream of drowning in the ocean and saw my dead father's body at the bottom. Was my fate to join him in a sea of unworthiness and lying in a great void for eternity?

"'When John was born, a phenomenon occurred. He was the spitting image of my beloved father! I needed a miracle, and when I looked into my son's eyes, I realized that I had just created one.

"'Now I had the chance to make amends for all the injustices my father endured. I could love him unconditionally and protect him from the scorn and disdain of the world. I could shield him from my mother's belittling. I could make him feel worthwhile. I could renew my father's eternal bond with myself!'

"When she ended her spiel, she slapped me across the face.

"'Mama,' she snarled at me, her daughter. 'Why did you treat Papa like that? You made his life miserable, and I couldn't save him.'

"Suddenly she gained her whereabouts, realized her mistake, and put her head down. 'I'm so sorry, Rose. I lost myself.'

"'But, forget John? How could I ever do that? It is the same as giving up and forgetting my dear father.

"'I'm sorry, Rose, but I am forever caught up in the past. John is like my father reborn, and you are the spitting image of my mother!

"'Please go. I cannot let go of the past. John is the reincarnation of my father, and you are the ghost of my mother.'

"And so I went!"

CHAPTER TWENTY-SEVEN

Cynthia – knowing and liking Rose's mother, Esther – didn't know how to respond. She certainly didn't want to take sides or diminish Rose's feelings, so she tried to get Rose to speak of happier times.

She asked Rose to continue her Woodstock story. She thought to herself, *Those were happy times for this emotionally torn woman.*

After a few moments, Rose composed herself and asked, "Do you really want to hear the rest of the story from forty years ago?"

Cynthia genuinely said, "Of course I do. You were at the center of an historical event. Please, tell me the rest of it! Did anything ever evolve with you and Jimmy?"

"Well, the rest of festival was great. It rained, we were dirty, we were stoned, we probably smelled like hell, but we were in love. Well at least for the next few months.

"After the Sly and the Family Stone set, we slept until noon the next day. We were wrapped up in a sleeping bag in the middle of a hill surrounded by 400,000 others, but we were content. I felt like staying that way forever, but eventually our friends woke us up.

ONE HUNDRED YEARS WITHOUT LOVE

"They fed us some granola that people were handing out and we smoked some weed. At about 2:00 pm on Sunday, the music started again. Joe Cocker, Country Joe and the Fish, Ten Years After. We held hands and hugged and kissed the whole time. It felt so natural, and I had never felt that way before!

"About eight that night, Jimmy's friends pulled him over and they started talking. Jimmy kept shaking his head and looking at me. I could see his face tighten up and his brow wrinkled in despair. What was going on? Were his friends telling him that I was not good enough for him? Did they think I was a one-night stand and should be tossed away? Were they telling him I was ugly or stupid? Was I delusional to think that anybody could fall in love with me?

"My heart was pounding, and the usual sensation of inferiority was settling in. I put my head down, and the tears started flowing. A few minutes later, Jimmy came over and tapped me on the shoulder. I couldn't bear to look at him and hear the forthcoming rejection.

"'Rose, I have to go now. My friends are leaving and that is my only way home. I'm so sorry; I was having the best time of my entire life!'

"There was an extended pause, and Jimmy seemed nervous. My heart missed a few beats during that silence.

"'Can we see each other again? Can I have your number and see you back home? We really don't live that far from each other.'

"I lifted my hands from my face and looked into the eyes of my angel. This was the first person that seemed infatuated with me, and I felt love like never before. I tried to answer, but the words were hard to get out. How do you respond the first time someone professes desire and love for you?

"Jimmy seemed nervous as I just stared at him. I can't imagine what he thought of this crazy non-responsive seventeen-year-old kid. I was filthy with ripped, wet clothing, and God only knows what I smelled like.

"He just grabbed my face, gazed into my eyes and gave me the most passionate kiss I ever had. My heart melted and I felt sensations that were foreign to me.

"He said I was the sunshine in this cloudy, rainy place. 'You have given me the best weekend of my life. This concert wasn't my style, but you made it special! Please see me again!'

"Without thinking, my impulse for being loved took over. I jumped up, grabbed his face and kissed his inviting lips. I wrapped my legs around his waist, and the momentum knocked us both over. After an initial thud and exclamation of 'What the fuck,' we both started laughing.

"We were kissing and hugging for about five minutes until one of his friends said, 'Okay, lover boy, we need to get going. Rose, can you give your new boyfriend your number so we can pry him away?'

"Embarrassed at this intrusion and obvious spectacle we'd created, we got up, exchanged numbers, and said our farewells. I was upset for the moment, as my first true love was leaving, but my heart was enlightened for the future."

Both Rose and Cynthia wiped the tears from their eyes.

CHAPTER TWENTY-EIGHT

"I know this is a little forward, and I'd understand if you don't want to talk about it, but what happened with you and Jimmy?"

Rose was quiet and seemed to contemplate this question. With apparent sadness she replied, "I have been through years of therapy and many tearful nights trying to answer that question.

"The short answer is we did, in fact, see each other after Woodstock. The long answer is that we married, got divorced, and remarried until he was taken away on 9/11."

Cynthia put her hand to her mouth in shock. She thought to herself, *What did she just say? Married, divorced, remarried, and taken away by Osama bin Laden on 9/11?*

Rose started telling the story. "Jimmy called me the very next day to see if I got home safely. Oh, when that phone rang and my mom yelled out, 'Rose, you have a phone call,' my heart skipped a beat. In anticipation. I ran downstairs. It was Jimmy, and I was so excited.

"If I had died right at that moment, it would have been a happy death. This stranger who I just met a few days ago couldn't wait to see me again. While most seventeen-year-old girls would be excited, years later my therapist suggested this was the love that I'd never really received before.

"She said to me, 'All human beings want and need to be loved. As a matter of fact, most of us are seeking it every day. Whether it is relationship love, parental love, status love, or something else, we strive for acceptance and adoration. Jimmy was perhaps the only person besides your father to provide you with it, or at least proclaimed it. Of course you were excited.'

"We met the following Saturday at Flushing Meadow Park in Queens. Upon seeing him, I uncontrollably ran up to him, smiled, and squeezed his hand.

"'Well, Rose, it's good to see you too, but could you ease up on your grip? You're breaking my hand!'

"Embarrassed, I let go and apologized. "I'm just so happy to see you; I guess I got carried away. Here, let me kiss your hand,' which I reflexively did.

"It's funny how different he looked from Woodstock. At Woodstock his hair was disheveled, he was dirty from the mud, and he had facial fuzz. He was now clean-shaven, well dressed, and nerdier looking.

"I was taken aback by this new Jimmy, and I took an abnormally long time looking him over.

"He stared at me and noticed I was drawing back and scanning him. 'What's the matter, Rose? Am I assuming too much? I thought we really hit it off at the festival last week.'

"After scrutinizing this new look and trying to match this Jimmy with Woodstock Jimmy, I concentrated solely on his eyes. They were indeed the same, and my heartbeat quickened. I broke out in a sweat and felt the same euphoria I'd felt at Woodstock.

"The love I'd experienced the previous weekend was two feet from my heart and soul. My lips moved toward the bewildered Jimmy, and I kissed and embraced him with no restraints. I was all in!

ONE HUNDRED YEARS WITHOUT LOVE

"At first, he seemed taken aback by my passion, but he relaxed and returned my affection. We made out for a long time, and finally, he stepped back and said, 'Well, I guess you still like me.'

"He grabbed my eager hand, and we started strolling around the park. I mentioned that I was a little surprised at his straight–laced appearance.

"'Well, we all were a little different last weekend. I mean half the crowd was probably stone heads and hippies. The other half were kids just going to a concert and having a good time. I learned a lot that weekend.

"'If half a million people from different backgrounds can get together and live in peace for three days amongst rain, drugs, lack of food, lack of bathroom facilities, how different can people be. While the older generation looks down on how the hippies and rebellious people might be, they are wrong. Wars rage, race riots occur, poverty is prevalent, but we younger people came together for peace, love, and acceptance.

"'I also learned to let my hair down, relax, and enjoy myself, rather than plan my future and try to make lots of money.

"'Most importantly, I met you and experienced a relationship that I wish to continue. I felt a connection to you at first sight. Do you like the real Jimmy?'

"I just nodded my head and looked into his eyes. 'Do you like the Queens Rose?'

"He drew me in, kissed me passionately, and whispered in my ear, 'I love the Queens Rose.'

"Love, love, love. Did he say the word love? I searched my memories. Had anybody ever told me they loved me?

"My memory drew a blank, and I was very quiet. We walked hand in hand around the lake as Jimmy pointed out the birds, turtles, trees and sights along the way.

"I wasn't really paying attention to the conversation. I shook my head and replied yeah every so often, but my thoughts were elsewhere. *This person loves me.*

"We made our way to the Unisphere, a huge steel monument built for the 1964 World's Fair. Jimmy asked me if I'd visited the World's Fair and I replied, 'No, my parents never really took us anywhere.'

"'Oh, that's too bad. Tell me about your family.'

"I just replied, 'I'd rather not. There really isn't much to tell anyway. Other than my father who isn't around much, they really don't treat me very well. I'd rather concentrate on this nice day and seeing you again. Let's not spoil the moment.'

"'Okay,' he stammered. 'To the present and the future then!'

"We walked, talked, and made out the rest of the afternoon. I returned home on a cloud!"

CHAPTER TWENTY-NINE

Rose's whole demeanor seemed to brighten as she rehashed her story of Jimmy. Both Cynthia and Molly were transfixed by the stronger and happier sounding voice. Nonetheless, Cynthia could detect a slight sadness in Rose's tone.

"Oh, those were good times for a while. You know dear, they say your first love will never leave you, even if the relationship fails. For me, not only was it my first boyfriend, it was the first time I felt unique and that someone other than my father really cared for me.

"Anyway, Jimmy and I saw each other every weekend and talked frequently by telephone. Oh, by the way, we didn't have today's fancy cell phones back then, so we kept our conversations quick as others could hear. My mother showed only a casual interest in my new boyfriend.

"You would think a mother would want to meet the boyfriend and know all the details. Oh, not my mother.

"Yet if John went on a date, she needed to know who the girl was and everything about her. I was so used to this nonchalant interest that I wasn't aware of the long-term effects on me.

"Jimmy invited me to meet his parents for dinner at their house in Forest Hills Gardens. With uneasiness I accepted, but

I was nervous as hell. What should I wear? What if they didn't like me? Would Jimmy ditch me if they didn't approve?

"Oh, my self-esteem was very fragile at the time. It had improved with having a steady boyfriend, but what if this dinner went poorly?

"I confided my nervousness to Jimmy, but he just reassured me. 'Rose, you are perfect; how could they not like you?' He bent down and kissed my nervous lips.

"'Oh, just to be sure, if you do something inappropriate, I will gently kick you under the table. Also, don't wear your ripped jeans or a tight top. Also, please don't chew gum or talk while you're eating. Please don't talk about politics or religion. My father is a conservative Republican, and mom is a religious nut. They are also very protective of me, so they will ask a lot of questions. Be prepared!'

"After that little pep talk, I was totally scared shitless.

"Jimmy didn't own a car, so I took the subway from Brooklyn to Queens. In those days the fare was twenty cents, and you used a metallic token; not one of those fancy cards they use these days. I had never been to this part of Queens before; I was a Brooklyn girl.

"It seemed like a different world to me. The houses and apartments weren't stacked on top of each other. They were large with expansive lawns and ornate gardens. The streets were lined with beech and birch trees reaching to the sky. Perhaps the strangest thing about this area of Queens was the lack of noise and scarcity of people. You could hear the birds singing and the children giggling. What a change from the honking of horns and the subway noise from Brooklyn. What kind of people lived here?

"After a short time, I found the address, and with trepidation I walked up the long, flowered pathway. The front door was a huge wrought iron double door twice my size. If Jimmy's parents' goal was to intimidate me, they succeeded! I started to sweat, and my heart began to race. 'What have I gotten myself into?'

"As I was about to ring the lighted bell, the door swung open.

"'Oh, you must be Rose. I am Jimmy's mother, Claire. Please come in.'

"As she opened the door and I stepped into the large, dark hallway, my heart rate went supersonic. Where was Jimmy? I fully expected him to greet me and make the introductions.

"Claire directed me towards an expansive, ornate living room. There were huge, old, European paintings of landscapes and canals in Germany. A grandfather clock chimed as I was guided to a huge, flowered couch. With a shy, squeaky voice, I timidly asked where Jimmy was.

"His mother softly answered that *James* was running a little errand and would be back shortly. 'I thought we could chat for a little while, Rose. Would you like a cup of tea?'

"Shaken that Jimmy wasn't there and the way she emphasized his full name, I perceived danger.

"'Rose, how old are you? You look so young.'

"I stammered, 'Almost eighteen.' She shook her head ever so slightly in the negative as the interrogation started.

"'So you and James met at that crazy concert last month.' I just quietly nodded my head as she continued. 'You know, I told James to go out and have some fun, but I never imagined he would go to a place like that! From the news reports and tapes, it looks like a group of hippies and gang members doing drugs, running around naked, and doing all sorts of crazy things. My James is a nice boy from a good family with a bright future ahead. Are you one of those hippy freaks?'

"Caught totally off guard, I just stammered, 'No, no. I went with my friend for a weekend of music and met Jimmy there. Nothing crazy went on between us. There was some weird stuff going on, but our little group just enjoyed the music and hung out. Jimmy and I developed a friendship and decided to see each other afterwards.

"I weakly stammered, 'When will Jimmy be back?'

"'Oh, he will be back soon. I just wanted to have a little alone time with you. You know, James has never had a girlfriend before, and he is really a little naïve. He is my only son, and I just wanted to make sure he met the *right* girl. Oh, men can be so stupid sometimes; they have animal instincts, you know. They might do anything or see anybody for sex.'

"With that she looked me right in the eye and accusingly asked, 'Did you and James have sex at the concert?'

"In disbelief at that question, I hesitated. I must have turned bright red with embarrassment, and I broke out into a sweat. Still processing the question, I thought to myself, *Did this woman just ask me if I had sex with her son?*

"We both locked eyes and I could feel the animosity from this total stranger. I lowered my gaze but still felt her eyes boring into my soul. I could sense she knew the answer. What should I do?"

Rose turned to Cynthia, who was totally absorbed and her pupils fully dilated. "Cynthia, what would you have done?"

Cynthia responded, "I can't believe anyone would ask that question to a young girl they had just met. Oh, my God; that is just shameful. What did you do?"

Rose responded, "Just out of curiosity, and because I still can't believe what I did, what would you have done?"

Cynthia thought for a few seconds and responded, "I probably would have lied like the dickens and said, 'Of course not.'"

Rose took a deep dejected breath and said, "That's how my friends and shrink responded. Well, my answer was a little different. I did what I did, and I don't regret it.

"That woman, rest her soul, deserved it. I was a young, teenaged girl in a strange area trying to be nice and meet my boyfriend's parents.

"Well, possessing the Shapiro genes, I raised my head, put my hands on my hips, locked eyes with her, and walked to within inches of that bitch.

"'Of course we did. As a matter of fact, we fucked our brains out and we enjoyed it!'

"Claire turned white as a ghost and her eyes glared maliciously at me. I could sense the rage at my bluntness, but I was so enraged that this total stranger would ask me that question that I attacked.

"I continued my onslaught. I lied and said, "Oh, by the way I may be pregnant. I guess that would make you a grandmother and force *Jimmy* to marry me. Maybe we can move into your house with the baby.

"Jimmy's mother turned five shades of white and covered her face. She leaned to the left and fainted dead away. Luckily, she was sitting on the couch and ended up lying sideways but out cold.

"Enraged at the interrogation from this woman, I didn't bother to see if she needed help. I got up, stormed out the front door, and left.

"As I walked the streets, I suddenly burst into tears. What had I just done? Sure, Claire was a rude, obnoxious, middle-aged bitch; but what of my relationship with Jimmy?

"My boyfriend would surely dump me after I insulted his mother like that. Would I ever find someone to love and be with again? Oh, that damn temper of mine! I imagined a life of darkness and loneliness as I stumbled my way towards the subway.

"Through the haze of tears, the walk back was different than before. The houses were monstrosities of cold brick and mortar. Through the windows, the inhabitants were ogres and demons. The trees and leaves appeared evil and threatening one's very existence. The playing children were killing animals and destroying property. The neighborhood was the devil's playground. Now I knew what kind of people lived there.

"I cried all night and nobody in my house even noticed. I eventually fell asleep, but my dreams had turned into nightmares."

CHAPTER THIRTY

Cynthia was stunned at Rose's story. She asked herself if she would have reacted in the same manner. *Nah, I don't have the nerve or the courage to confront anybody like that.* The only other person that would probably have acted like that was Rose's mother, Esther.

Nervously she asked Rose, "Did Jimmy ever contact you again?"

Rose smiled and replied, "Well, we were married for almost thirty years with a break in the middle. We have a daughter together who is married and lives in Colorado. So, I guess the answer would be yes.

"Not that our relationship was a bed of roses, my dear. Our first marriage was stormy to say the least. Two weeks went by after that fiasco without a word from Jimmy. I was too scared to call and certain he would never speak to me again.

"Who knew what happened after the incident? Maybe his mother died or had a stroke or ordered him to never see me again. Remember, I was only seventeen and looking back, a naïve, stupid girl from blue collared Brooklyn.

"I started to ease Jimmy out of my future when the doorbell rang one Sunday. I was in my bedroom, just moping around in clothes that I hadn't changed in days. My hair was like a wild tumbleweed, and my face was filthy. Suddenly I heard my mother shriek out, 'Rose, there is someone here to see you!'

"I really didn't feel like seeing my friend, Jill, who occasionally came over when she was bored. She was an only child and like me, had poor self-esteem. Times with her consisted of whining about our bad luck and complaining that life sucked.

"I dragged my disheveled self down the steps, trying to decide if I was up to hanging out with Jill. I really wasn't in the mood for anything but solitude and self-pity. I'd had my one shot at love and I messed up!

"I wish I had a picture of my reaction when I saw Jimmy at the base of the stairs. He had one red rose held up to his heart and raised it towards me.

"My mother smiled and stepped into another room. I froze at this surprise and didn't know which way to run. I covered up my face, half in disbelief and half to cover up my disastrous appearance.

"Jimmy, sensing my uneasiness asked, 'Rose can we talk?'

"Without waiting for a reply, he continued. 'I'm so sorry for not being there when you arrived at my house. Believe me, that was not my intention. I was tricked into not being there. Please give me a chance to explain!'

"I started to open my mouth, but he continued with his apology.

"'I can't even begin to imagine what happened. I don't for one second believe what mom said about you. I care for you very much and would love to spend time with you.'

"I stammered, 'Jimmy, I didn't expect to see you again. Oh, I must look like an ugly witch right now. Can you give me a few minutes to change and make myself presentable?'

ONE HUNDRED YEARS WITHOUT LOVE

"He nodded his head, and I ran back up the stairs. With a pounding heart, I scurried about changing clothes, scrubbing my face and combing my mess of hair. A few moments later, my mother walked into my room and smiled. 'Rose, who is that boy?'

"'Oh, just some boy I met at the concert a few months ago.'

"'Just some boy? He seems mighty infatuated by you. Have you been seeing him regularly?'

"'Well, maybe a few times since then, but we had a falling out. I didn't expect him to just pop in like this.'

"'That's okay, Rose. He looks like a nice young man and appears to be quite smitten with you. I was starting to get concerned about the dating thing with you. It's good to see you with a nice boy and not doing drugs or whatever these hippie people do.'

"I thought to myself, *You should have seen me at Woodstock*. I said, 'Mom, this is not the best time for a conversation like this. Maybe if you cared, you'd talk to me a little more.'

"My mom looked surprised and replied, 'You're right. We should talk more.' She walked out, and I noticed her wiping tears from her cheek. I sensed a sign of regret from Mom, but I didn't dwell on it.

"What the hell was Jimmy doing here? Was it to say goodbye? His mom probably forbade him from seeing me.

"Was he still interested in seeing me? He brought a red rose. My heart threatened to jump out of my body.

"After fixing myself up, I walked down the stairs to Mom and Jimmy talking. I was nervous about what she may say, or Jimmy judging our meager house and furniture. Jimmy's eyes lit up when he saw me, and he said, 'Rose, can we please talk? I have a lot of explaining to do.'

"Mom took the hint and left the room with a huge grin on her face. I sat next to Jimmy and put my head down. I couldn't look at him.

"Suddenly, he grabbed my hands and lifted my chin. To say I was startled would be the ultimate understatement. Imagine my situation: an unloved, lonely, seventeen-year-old girl who went through that trauma with her first boyfriend's mother just two weeks earlier.

"Not having heard from him for two weeks, I was certain my first and maybe only boyfriend had dumped me, and I was back to being worthless again.

"I have since realized that our own self-esteem is from within, not dependent on what others think. But my seventeen-year-old self was totally dependent on other people's opinions! Without true parental love I was a nobody!

"'Rose, I'm so sorry for not seeing you sooner. It appears my mother engineered that day to drive you away. You see, my mom and dad want me to marry only a German girl with a prestigious background. They want me to climb the business ladder and be a rich, successful accountant. When they discovered you were a Jewish girl from Brooklyn, they freaked.

"'They manipulated both of us into breaking up. I'm so, so sorry it took me two weeks to be man enough to stand up to them. After these past two weeks of reflection, and to be honest, loneliness, I decided to rebel. I know I will catch all hell, but God damn it, it is my life!

"'As I left the house this morning with this rose, my mother asked, "Are you going to see that girl who tried to kill me?"

"'Mom, she did not try to kill you! She simply stood up to your outrageous grilling of her and her character. Unlike dad and me, she actually had the nerve to stand up to you.

ONE HUNDRED YEARS WITHOUT LOVE

Do you want me to marry a lamb being led to slaughter or a strong independent woman? I know your answer, but that girl – whose name is Rose – and I may be in love. I only hope she will forgive me for your actions and my inactions. She may not be German or from a wealthy family, but she is an amazing girl. She has more substance and moral character than you could imagine. I am twenty-two years old and don't have to listen to you or Father and have my life controlled.

"'If you choose to live a loveless life in luxury and stature, so be it. I choose to live my life with someone I love regardless of nationality, race, or status.

"'I slammed the door as I left. My mother appeared so upset, I wouldn't be surprised if she changed the locks on the doors.

"'Rose, can you forgive me? I love you and want to spend more time with you. Maybe even the rest of our lives together! What do you think? Can you forgive me for the past two weeks? Can we start fresh?'

"My heart was pounding, and I was sure all could hear it, but I played hard to get. My response was, 'I suppose we can try it again, but my feelings were really hurt. I don't know if I can give myself as freely as before. To be honest, I have had so much rejection in my life, I'm afraid! Do you mind if we take things slowly?'

"Jimmy looked at me in despair and lowered his head. 'I understand, Rose. Please just remember, it was my parents, not me, who almost broke us up. It is true that I was a weak weasel for not marching right over and apologizing. I guess after all those years of being bossed by my mother, I didn't have the courage to defy her. Damn her meddling!

"'I promise you from now on, you are my number one girl and she is just my mom!' He leaned forward and gave me a powerful kiss. Against my better judgment, I gave into my emotions and hormones and returned his affections with added fervor."

Cynthia smiled as she envisioned a young Rose beaming with the intensity of a first love. She remembered her own mother telling her, *There are many kinds of love in this world, but you will never experience the same love twice.*

Cynthia's imagination was able to erase Rose's wrinkles, eye bags, and gray hair. In her place was an innocent, clear skinned, radiant teenager with a well-formed body bursting with enthusiasm.

She looked up, and just like with Esther, the leaves appeared to rise and reattach to the old oak tree. Cynthia thought to herself, *I must be delusional, but nature seems to reverse its aging when these two relive their past! Amazing!*

CHAPTER THIRTY-ONE

Rose continued. "Jimmy and I resumed our weekly dating, and I slowly let my guard down. I wouldn't let him get as physical with me as at Woodstock, but we did hold hands and talked about our lives.

"Jimmy was an only child raised in a strict German household. His father was rarely home as he was an important bank manager in Manhattan. His mother ran a tight ship around the house and set limits on Jimmy's behavior.

"'Rose, believe me, when a German mother tells you how to act, you do it! No discussions or arguments! My father is able to keep me obedient by just staring at me. With his austere appearance, no words are necessary. I'm reminded constantly that I come from good stock and most residents of Queens and Brooklyn are poor, dirty foreigners. They tell me I should stay with my own kind and be studious. My parents expect great things from me, and I must limit distractions. According to my mother, *distractions* means liberals that are rebelling against the government. She says that anti-war radicals and civil rights advocates are nothing but trouble. She also insists I have nothing to do with trampy girls who want rich guys or are loose in their sexual morals. Some girls will do anything to get the right man.

"'She's sure that when the time is right, we will find me a *suitable* young wife. She will be tall, blond, strong, and smart like our people usually are.' Jimmy rolled his eyes as he recounted his mother's demands.

"'She tells me that she's sure my future wife will support my career, bear me children, and if I'm lucky, be good in the bedroom. Then I can indulge in things that men lust!'

"Jimmy continued, 'When I was sixteen and I became interested in girls, I asked if I could go to a boy-girl party. My mother's face became stone cold, and I thought she would slap me.'

"'She insisted I was too good for something like that. She didn't want me to be mingling with the wrong types of people, as she put it, which included young tarts hoping to get laid or hippie friends spending all night getting high.

"'I assured her it was only a small get together, watching TV. We wouldn't be having wild sex or doing drugs, or whatever she thought non-German kids did. I told her I wanted to hang out with girls and find my own love.'

"'But she was insistent that an arranged marriage was more practical than love. Love was for fairy tales. Wars, killings, infidelities are about this imaginary thing called love. In her view, most marriages weren't about love. Most married people didn't even know the meaning. They were just conveniences between a man and a woman to have children and avoid loneliness. Society pressured women to marry for support, protection, and someone to put them in a family way. Spinsters are looked down upon and few die happily.

"He continued to tell me all about what his mother thought about marital relationships. 'Men, on the other hand, are considered successful if they have a prestigious job and money. They need sex like flowers need the sun. Give a man sex once a week, feed him well, clean his house, and raise his children. That is all men really need and want.

"'If a woman is very lucky, her husband will remain loyal after the children are older. If not, the husbands take mistresses and come home late all the time.

"'She insisted that even though her words seemed cruel, they were the truth. She assured me that my father was a good man who provided her a nice house and all the material benefits she wanted. With me to raise, she has been satisfied. The only thing she wished for more of was children, but she told me that my father was always too busy.'

"Jimmy continued, "'Rose, my mom, for the only time that I can remember, totally let her guard down. That authoritative, emotionless German mother put her head down and became quiet. She sniffled a few times, regained some composure and uttered repressed truths.

"'She told me that my father had had numerous affairs! Affairs with his secretary, colleagues, and clients. She said they were all younger, prettier, and had better figures than her.

"'She cursed herself for getting older and losing her looks. She hated her wrinkles and was convinced her figure had gone to pot.

"'But she consoled herself with the thought that he was home each night with a peck on the cheek and sleeping in her bed. She hated his infidelities but had made the decision to just put up with it. She insisted it was a successful marriage, though not one that included love.

"'She told me that I was her one true joy in life. That's why she was so overprotective and wanted to choose my wife herself. She couldn't bear to let me marry someone she deemed unworthy to take her only child away!'

"I was spellbound by the story and delighted that Jimmy was confiding in me. For him to tell me these intimate details meant he felt free and wanted to share his life with me. Was this love?

"Jimmy continued, 'Through most of my life, I did exactly as I was expected to do. I went to a private all boys' school. I played and hung out with friends my mother chose and stayed away from girls. When I would instinctually peek at a pretty girl, Mom gave me a stern look. But when I went to St. John's University, my world expanded!

"'It was at St. John's that I discovered Mom's teachings were very restrictive and actually backwards. There were so many kids from other backgrounds and different ethnicities that I experienced a shocking revelation. There were black kids, brown kids, Asian kids, religious Jewish kids, Irish kids, and few German American kids. At first, I was apprehensive as Mom and Dad belittled and warned me that they were inferior. I tried to distance myself from these strange people, but soon through labs and breakout groups I was forced to interact with them.

"'My initial trepidation diminished as I learned they were nice, intelligent, well-behaved people. They went out of their way to help and befriend me. My mistrust soon turned to free interaction and eventual friendship. I learned a lot from these interactions.

"'Not all kids had parental marriages similar to mine. In fact, some kids were fatherless, some had stepparents, many had divorced parents, and many more had multiple siblings.

"'I saw some parents dropping their kids off and hugging and displaying affection. Some of the college kids had girlfriends and boyfriends and made out all over the place.

Many waited outside the others classroom and grabbed each other's hands. Love seemed to be in the air.

"'Many of the kids, including the Caucasians, wore long disheveled hair and some girls went braless. They hung out in groups and discussed how Presidents Johnson and Nixon had been deceiving the American people about the Vietnam War. We were in fact, not winning that war, and there were civilian casualties inflicted by our forces.

"'A taboo subject in my house was the civil rights movements and social unrest. These subjects were all over the campus. They had signs all over the walls demanding equal rights for all."

"Asian kids were prevalent, and they were in fact very intelligent, well-mannered, nice people. There were Jewish kids dressed strangely wearing yarmulkes, but studious and very smart. I began to wonder how Mom could say all those bad things about these different but normal people.

"'The truth was, they are more real than my parents! Dad dressed well and was proper but was also very superficial and only interested in money. Mom acted like a Queen and considered most others inferior to her. She was secretly called the German monarch of Forest Hills.

"'I slowly started joining clubs and hanging out with the rabble. We discussed the Vietnam War, the older generation, and having a good time. Most of them demeaned the older generation as being materialistic and out of touch with nature, their true feelings, and giving to others.

"'I started hanging out on campus after classes and listening to music, arguing about the professors and making friends. We went to restaurants, and I had Chinese food, Italian food, and foods I never heard of before. My life opened, but I was still very shy around girls. I must have had, and still have, suppressed inhibitions brought on by my disapproving mother.

"'Rose, you are the first and only girl I ever really kissed, and as you may have noticed at Woodstock, I was a little inexperienced at love making.'"

CHAPTER THIRTY-TWO

Rose shook her head at the mere memory of Jimmy's admission before continuing her story. "'I suspected that it was your first time.'

"Jimmy blushed and we both giggled. 'I'm sure I can do better the second time if you'd give me a chance.'

"I stepped back, put my arms out, and gently pushed him away. 'Not so fast, mister. This is not Woodstock. A month ago, I was ridiculed at your parents' house and didn't hear from you for two whole weeks! I was so depressed and brokenhearted that I actually thought about ending it all. Even though it was not my first time being with a boy in that way, it was the first time I felt romantically involved. I truly believed I had finally found someone who loved me for who I truly was. I know that may sound like a young immature infatuation, but to me it was reality.'

"Jimmy dropped his head in embarrassment as I continued. 'You are not the only one raised in a screwed up family. I am, and always have been, second fiddle to my brother. My mother basically ignores me without actually voicing it. I know she doesn't really like me.'

"I remember feeling the tears welling in my eyes, but acknowledging my mother's preference for John quickly made me angry rather than sad. 'Believe me, it is not just my imagination; everybody else knows it. I'm not looking for anybody's pity, but it is an explanation of who I am. I can put up with being yelled at and being treated poorly, but to be ignored is the worst. I have always felt guilty of being a pathetic excuse for a daughter and unworthy of being loved. My life, until I met you, was just a downward spiral with little hope of getting out. I was going through the motions of life without any direction.

"'When I met you, my whole perspective changed. For that time period when we were going out, I had a refreshed spirit! I looked forward to waking up to a day in which I felt loved. The sky seemed bluer, the trees were greener, the flowers smelled fresher, and food was tastier. I went to sleep peacefully rather than agonizing about how cruel life could be. But that abruptly changed!'

"There was a full minute of silence after my speech.

"'Oh, why did you let me walk into your house to face your mother alone? Where were you? You left me totally unprepared for her verbal abuse. Why did you invite me over to meet your parents when you knew they wouldn't approve of me? If you truly like, love, or want to be with me you should have been there. It was you that invited me, after all. I needed you. Goddamit, where were you?'

"With tears welling in his eyes, Jimmy apologized. 'I'm so, so sorry, Rose. But my intentions were true. I wanted to show my parents how nice you were and how much I cared for you. I was very hopeful we could convince them to accept you, and for that matter, us as a couple. Rose, I was manipulated and tricked into not being there!'

ONE HUNDRED YEARS WITHOUT LOVE

"I could barely believe my ears. 'What the hell are you talking about? What kind of idiot do you think I am? How can you be tricked into being away for a dinner that you arranged?'

"Jimmy just kind of hung his head down, and his complexion went from pale to ghostly. He started to tap his fingers together as if deciding to let out a big secret. My heart accelerated in anticipation of bad news. Had he gotten sick? Had he been in an emergency room? What was it that prevented him from being there?

"He finally stammered out, 'Well, I hate to badmouth my mother, but she tricked me. When I told her you were a Jewish girl from Brooklyn, she shook her head and said NO WAY!

"'I put my foot down and informed her that I was seeing you whether she approved or not. I told her how wonderful you were and that we were probably in love! If she refused to accept this relationship, I was ready to move out and give up my inheritance.

"'Well, you should have seen the look on her face after my declaration. I had never witnessed her speechless and apparently defeated. I felt like a true man at that moment, finally giving commands instead of obeying them. She relented and agreed to meet you. I should have suspected she wouldn't give in so easily.

"'About one hour before you were due to arrive, the house phone rang. After a few minutes, I heard mother walk up the stairs to my bedroom. She knocked on the door and entered.'"

"She told me you were running behind, that you'd had some kind of family emergency, and would be at least an hour late. Mother says she told you to just come whenever you could, and then asked me to go to the deli in Rego Park to get some knishes and Jewish cookies to make you feel more comfortable when you arrived.

"'I was surprised that Mom hadn't conferred with me, but much appreciated her apparent kindness to you. Maybe she knew that I was deadly serious and didn't want to estrange her only son.

"'I thanked her for being so nice and hurried off to the deli. It was about a mile away, but since I was told you would be an hour late, I had plenty of time to get the food and be back.

"'During that walk, I felt my world finally coming together. I had a comfortable family life, nice friends, and enjoyed my new job. Yet, there was something missing. I think that missing part was you!

"'But when I came back, it was all over!'

"Upon hearing the story and the sincerity in his voice, I caved in. I realized that I too was searching for someone to feel that way about me all my life. To finally find that person and believe in it was music to my ears.

"My heart and mind believed Jimmy's story and the barriers that I created came tumbling down! Jimmy and I had the most romantic night of our young lives.

"We were married two years later despite Jimmy's parents' disapproval.

"Alas, I was still very young and overly clingy. We had our ups and downs like most marriages, but my insecurities proved too much for him to bear. While inwardly I know he loved me, we divorced after a few years."

Cynthia's excitement of hearing of Rose marrying her Jimmy quickly turned to despair when she learned of the divorce.

With a look and sound of sadness, Rose nonetheless cracked a sly small smile.

"We remarried three years after the divorce! I guess true love conquers the imperfections in us all. It appears that Jimmy really loved this imperfect human being."

Cynthia put her arms to her chest and shed a tear.

Impishly, Rose cracked a smile and laughed. "Or we were two screwed up young people looking for the love we were denied growing up. I'd since come to believe we were about love and not need!

"We became a happy married couple with obvious quirks and eventually we had a child together. While I still had a contemptuous relationship with my mother, I was, for the most part, happy."

Suddenly Rose put her head down and started crying. Between heaves and sobs she managed to gasp out, "All that ended on 9/11!"

CHAPTER THIRTY-THREE

Cynthia's emotions were riding a roller coaster. *Oh, my God,* she thought. *This woman could write a book.* Cynthia's mind flashed to the past.

She was in elementary school the day the world changed. At about 9:30 am on Tuesday, September 11, 2001, the principal interrupted classes and asked all the teachers to report to his office.

All of the children were bewildered by the adults' subsequent behavior. The teachers were all whispering, and some were crying. Everyone was eventually told that several planes had purposely crashed into buildings in Manhattan. 2,977 Americans were killed in those attacks, the Pentagon, and a field in Pennsylvania.

Victims were killed in various horrific manners. Most were incinerated instantaneously, others jumped to their deaths, while others were crushed during the collapses. It was the first and only time that the United States was attacked in the continental forty-eight states. To this day, people were still getting sick and dying from illnesses acquired by being near ground zero.

ONE HUNDRED YEARS WITHOUT LOVE

Teachers stopped teaching as they watched the television in the staff lounge. Many parents came to pick up their kids and everyone eventually learned that several parents had been killed in the attack.

When Cynthia returned home from school, she was shocked to see her father home. For the next two days her parents were glued to the television as all the channels were showing the destruction. The videos of people jumping to their deaths and the towers collapsing were forever engrained in her soul. The war in Afghanistan lasted twenty years as a result of that attack.

Cynthia was brought back to the present as Rose collected herself and told her story.

"At 10:28 am on September 11, 2001, both the north tower of the World Trade Center and my life collapsed! It had been burning for an hour and forty-two minutes and Jimmy never made it out!"

With her head down and in a melancholy tone, Rose continued, "Oh, what a beautiful day it started out to be. The sky was crystal clear, the air crisp, warm, and invigorating. Jimmy and I were living in a nice apartment in Park Slope, Brooklyn, that made for an easy commute to lower Manhattan. We both worked in Manhattan's financial district.

"I was a secretary for Merrill Lynch on the sixty-first floor of the South tower of the World Trade Center. Jimmy was a senior accountant for Bank of America on the ninety-fifth floor in the North Tower."

"It was such an ideal setup for us, as we usually commuted together and had a lunch date at least once a week. Everybody that worked in the towers had some trepidation of being so high up. There was also the lingering memory of a bomb explosion killing six people in 1993.

"When I started working there, I was both nervous and fascinated. I was a young woman from a poor Brooklyn neighborhood in a cosmopolitan building. The two main towers, which each contained 30,000 workers each day, was more than just a workplace. It was a really a city in itself. Most outsiders didn't know, but there were actually five other smaller buildings. There were parks and plazas to mingle outside, and periodically there were free concerts and Broadway specials. There were seven floors of retail shopping below ground level. There was even an art gallery.

"The elevators were so fast it was like an amusement park ride. The first few weeks I looked outside the huge windows every moment I could. Since we occupied the entire floor, you could see for miles in any direction. The Statue of Liberty and ferries scurrying tourists back and forth were a southern view. If you looked north, mid-Manhattan and Central Park appeared in the distance. New Jersey to the west and Brooklyn with its bridges to the east was exhilarating. You could see all the sightseeing boats and helicopters ferrying their patrons. From our vantage point the surrounding areas seemed like a living, moving dollhouse.

"They say that eventually you get used to your workplace and the initial thrill and trepidation fades. Well, that never happened to me. It really was a magical place to be, let alone work and earn a living there. The hustle and bustle of the area, along with the elegance of the towers themselves, made every day special."

Rose's face shined and her cheeks turned a rosy red. She was quiet for a while, and Cynthia surmised that she was reliving those good times.

ONE HUNDRED YEARS WITHOUT LOVE

Cynthia closed her eyes and tried to visualize the Twin Towers before that day. The towers appeared as two stately monuments representing the free world. She remembered seeing the movie *9/11: The Twin Towers*. As she visualized horrible scenes from that movie, her face blanched and she thought, *Oh my God. Rose was in one of those buildings.*

The wind kicked up for a moment, and several leaves brushed their faces.

Rose, brought back to the current time by the disturbing wind, continued. "After saying good-bye to Jimmy at the subway exit that morning, I bought my coffee at my regular stand. As I was a little early, I sipped my coffee outside and took in the fresh crisp air. The sky was cloudless and the early autumn air refreshing. Everybody seemed unusually relaxed and happily making his or her way into the buildings. It was probably the nicest day for the worst event ever to occur. As I entered the building, I noticed a squawking bluebird flying away.

"I got to my desk at exactly 8:30am. I slipped off my sneakers, put on my work shoes and flipped on my computer. As I checked my e-mails, I greeted my boss and co-workers as they walked by.

"Oh, the correspondence was the usual requests for statements and tax forms. Human resources were announcing some planned building safety drills that would occur in the following months.

"As I scanned the correspondence, a huge roar suddenly erupted at exactly 8:46. The windows shook, and the building actually swayed. We all looked at each other, wondering what had happened. One of the traders got up and pointed to the windows facing the North Tower.

"We all turned and saw the calamity unfolding. There were balls of fire, black smoke, and falling debris exploding from the sky. 'Holy shit!' someone exclaimed.

"We ran towards the window facing the North Tower and saw parts of a big plane jutting out from some of the higher floors in the North Tower. There were papers, furniture, and building debris fluttering downward. Bright yellow fire and black smoke were engulfing the floors above the area of impact.

"My heart sank, as I knew Jimmy was on the 95th floor of that building. While we didn't know exactly which floors had been hit, I knew it was close to Jimmy's office.

"Our manager, Jonathan Roth, speculated that a tourist plane had accidentally slammed into the building. He cursed at the idiot pilot that caused the crash. 'He probably killed a lot of people.' There was chaos as several women asked if they should evacuate our building.

"Jonathan reassured us that we were safe as it was undoubtedly an accident, and either way it wasn't our building. Confusion reigned until the building security announced that there was an incident at the North Tower. They assured us that we were unaffected and to remain on our floors. They would keep us up to date once they got more information.

"I uncontrollably shrieked out, 'But my husband is in that other building! Are they okay?'

"My friend, Anna, who knew Jimmy worked in the other Tower came, over and wrapped her arms around me. 'Don't worry, Rose. I'm sure it's a minor accident. Besides, it looks like it's lower than the 95th floor. That's where Jimmy works, right?'

"I nodded my head in affirmation and felt a glimmer of hope. Through the horror of the scene in front of me, I ignorantly believed Jimmy was alive. That hope is what kept me going as I barely made it out of our soon to be hit building.

"One of the older traders, Joe Sullivan, told a few of his nearest workers, 'I was here in '93 during that bombing. I'm getting the hell out of here! This could very well be an accident, but I'm not sticking around to find out. I would recommend we all leave RIGHT NOW!'

"His boss told him to remain at his desk and follow security's directive. Joe raised his middle finger and said, 'Do as you want. I'm getting out of here!'

"Chaos ensued with arguments split between staying and leaving. For me, I could not remain at my desk with Jimmy in that other burning building. I had to do something!

"About twenty of us followed Joe to the stairways and started making our way down the sixty-one flights of stairs. Joe, taking the lead, warned us not to take the elevators. 'I know it may be much quicker, but you don't want to be in an elevator during a terrorist attack!'

"By the way, if you think walking down steps is easy, you are wrong. Muscles you rarely use start aching and throbbing. Luckily it wasn't too crowded, and we were progressing well. I wasn't overly worried about my own safety; I was more concerned about Jimmy. This was a great excuse to get out and try to help him.

"I was aiding an older, overweight coworker, so my mind was somewhat occupied. If I knew Jimmy was burning up or dead, believe me, I wouldn't have tried so hard to get out.

"When we got to the forty-fifth floor, the public address system came alive and told us the situation was under control and to remain in place.

"Our leader at this time was Joe, and he declared, 'Bullshit. I'm not taking any chances. We should get the hell out of this deathtrap, wait outside, and see what develops.'

"Most of the group followed suit and continued our long trek down the World Trade Center South Tower. Three from our group threw up their arms, declared us crazy, and made their way to the elevators. They did not make it out!

"We were all getting a little tired and the pace slowed. We picked up a few strangers from other floors that had the same idea.

"When we hit the landing on the 31st floor, another even louder explosion erupted and the building shook. I was actually lifted off my feet and the whole building swayed back and forth! Luckily, I landed on my knees and quickly picked myself up. I had never been so scared in my life.

"The building was still swaying as we began to feel intense heat from above. Surely the building was falling over, and death was imminent. Even though I wasn't religious, I prayed to God to save me.

"With our hearts racing, the swaying slowly stopped but we remained frozen. I could hear Joe saying, 'See, I told you! This is a terrorist attack and that was not an accidental hit on the North Tower! Our building undoubtedly has just been hit by another plane. Come on! Let's get moving!'

"It took several seconds for his exclamation to settle in. *Is this for real? Are we really under attack? Is this building going to collapse with me inside?* I could feel my life flashing before my eyes.

"While some people recall their younger days from mental images, my memory was triggered by real photos. My therapist thought that I was repressing my childhood memories, as it was an unhappy one at best. She suggested that people with happy childhoods had better visual imagery than those without.

ONE HUNDRED YEARS WITHOUT LOVE

"The first picture to flash was me as baby in a family portrait. John, as a toddler, was on my mother's knee, and I was cradled by my father in a blanket.

"With whirlwind speed, old photos of my family flashed by. I noticed for the first time that Mom was usually holding John and smiling. When she was holding me, she appeared stern and detached.

"Images not triggered by photos flashed through my mind after Jimmy and I were a couple. The wedding and my honeymoon elicited a quick smile amongst the deathly fear of the moment.

"Before I came back to reality, I concluded that if Jimmy was dead my life was over either way. Photos would be all that was left of me. Neither John nor Mom would blink an eye if I didn't make it.

"The shaking of the building was replaced by dark smoke and the smell of jet fuel seeping from above. We hastened our descent, and soon the stairways became more crowded. The public address system was silent. We were totally on our own! There was some shrieking and crying, but for the most part there wasn't any pushing or a total free for all.

"My fear of dying changed from being burnt alive or a building collapse to a new concern: death by asphyxiation!

"The smoke became denser, and it was getting harder and harder to breathe. A few people stopped, moved to the side and developed coughing fits. My mundane, unfulfilled life would end up being just a statistic in tomorrow's news.

"When all seemed lost, we heard a new sound. At first it was very faint and appeared to be coming from below us. I thought to myself, *This must be part of the attack and we're trapped! Are we about to be gunned down?*"

"The noise grew louder, and it started to sound like footsteps. Soon voices could be heard and beams of light shined through the haze.

"We were trapped and people were actually backing up? Thoughts of my mother saying, 'I told you so,' popped into my head.

"Bullshit! You never told me anything, and now I am about to die!"

"As my eyes closed and I waited for the end, the voices from below bellowed, 'Come on, people! Keep it moving!'

"I reopened my eyes, and a flashlight beam momentarily blinded me. As I slowly regained some vision, I saw the most amazing sight! Appearing through the black smoke, spacemen with heavy suits on, flashlight in one hand and axes on the other, were moving towards us. I soon realized they were firefighters with eighty pounds of gear climbing up our stairwell.

"My surprise gave way to hope and then a realization. They were going the wrong way!

"In a moment, I grabbed one of their bulky arms and said, 'What are you doing? There is fire and smoke above. This building has been swaying and may very well collapse. You need to get out of here too!'

"The tall, exhausted, sweaty fireman looked me in the eye, and with an unbridled spirit said, 'Ma'am, this is our job. When we signed up, we took an oath that we were willing to give our life in the line of duty. I know that may seem crazy to you, and there is a chance I may not make it out alive, but we must save as many as we can. You best get moving along as I fear you may be right. There is a good chance this building may not hold up. That was a fully fueled jet plane that attacked this building and jet fuel is an intense fire. God be with you.'

ONE HUNDRED YEARS WITHOUT LOVE

"With that parting word, he continued his march along with many others to their deaths. 343 firefighters lost their lives that day. Many a family lost a father, brother, or son. To this day I praise every firefighter and policeman I encounter. Their bravery and dedication is unsurpassed.

"All of our group made it out before our tower collapsed. My beloved Jimmy never had a chance; he was on the floor that the first plane hit!"

CHAPTER THIRTY-FOUR

The final time Cynthia saw Rose was three days after their last meeting. Cynthia had been away for the weekend in the Poconos. The little getaway was a refreshing time for her hard-working husband and herself. While they delighted during this alone time, both seemed distracted. Cynthia's thoughts kept drifting back to Esther and Rose's life stories.

During their hikes, Cynthia was imagining living during the Great Depression, visiting sick people in a sanitarium, being at Woodstock in 1969, and being in Manhattan the morning of 9/11. She thought to herself, *Oh, the things that those women lived through.*

That Monday in November was called an Indian summer day. The temperature was in the high seventies and the sun was shining brightly. The birds were noisy as Molly and Cynthia made their way to the gardens.

Cynthia was very apprehensive. This might not be their typical routine of conversation and reliving the past. Three days had passed and hundred-year-old Esther may have passed away. For that matter, Rose may no longer be in New York or waiting for Cynthia at the garden.

The three women's lives had become intertwined. Cynthia was happier that she had made new friends and looked forward to their meetings. She was, in fact, fascinated by the older ladies' recollections of historical events that Cynthia had only read about.

She was mortified yet entranced by their emotional rollercoaster lives of feeling unloved. Were they victims of the times and circumstances or were they just a product of poor parenting? Perhaps they imagined and exaggerated things that simply weren't true. This was a Hallmark movie in real life.

Cynthia thought to herself, *I never realized the depth of how poor parenting could affect and damage lives.* These two older women had their entire beings molded by their parental upbringing. Even Esther at the ripe old age of one hundred, and Rose at over sixty carry these scars to this day.

Cynthia promised herself, *When I have children, I will treat them equally and demonstrate strong love every day. As I have always read, history is important as it allows us to learn and not repeat the mistakes of the past.*

Both Esther and Rose suffered immeasurably from lack of maternal love and being the least favored.

"That will not happen to my children!"

As she neared the gardens she felt her heart accelerate in anticipation. To her astonishment, Rose was sitting on the bench feeding some birds and wearing a colorful, flowered dress. Her hair was styled and immaculate, clipped back with a pretty barrette. A summer bonnet was perched atop her head.

As Cynthia approached the bench, she noticed that Rose was wearing makeup and appeared years younger. A smooth forehead replaced her previous frown lines, and she was smiling. The dark circles under her eyes were gone and her pupils were bright and shiny. She thought to herself, *Is this the same woman I saw three days ago?*

Before Cynthia could say a word, Rose jumped up like a teenager and hugged her. The embrace lasted an exceedingly long time, and Cynthia became nervous. "What is going on?"

"Oh, I'm so glad to see you! I thought that I might miss you as I'm going back to Chicago on Wednesday. There is so much to tell."

Cynthia's mouth popped open, and her facial contortion asked the question.

"Mom's funeral is tomorrow!"

Seeing Cynthia turn white and drop Molly, Rose covered her mouth. "Oh my, I am so stupid. My feeble mind isn't working clearly these days. I'm so sorry to spring the news to you that way; I know you and my mother had become close. Mom passed away on Saturday."

"Oh, I'm so sorry. You must feel awful, Rose. Is there anything I can do for you? You must be heartbroken."

"Thank you for the offer, but you have already done so much for my mom and myself. More than you can imagine. You were a good companion for her, and in the short time we have known each other, you have become a good and trusted friend.

"You know, I don't really feel that sad. Mom lived a full, if not the happiest, life possible. She had a loving father, sisters for companions, was married, and had two kids. That is more than many of us, including myself, have had.

"As a matter of fact, I am relieved in some respects. I knew she was suffering in both body and spirit. The only thing that could have lifted her spirits was seeing John. She had lost all her family and friends, and her body was on life support. I think she is in a better place now. I have a warm sensation in my body and soul that she is reunited with her family and reconciled with *her* mother."

Cynthia responded, "I hope you are right, but none of us will ever know."

"Oh, I have some inside information that my hunches are correct! Something strange happened the day she died. I never really put much faith in the spiritual world, but now I am a believer. Both John and I witnessed an unearthly event the other day."

Cynthia's mouth popped open. "Did you say John was there? I mean in New York, at your mother's bedside?"

With a huge grin Rose replied, "Yep, and he is still here until after the funeral.

"This past Saturday, the visiting nurse checked her vitals and nodded her head. She took me into the other room and informed me that all Mom's vital signs were bad and worsening quickly.

"'I'm afraid the end is very near and there is nothing else we can do. We can take her to a hospital, but that will not alter the inevitable. I recommend that we just leave her alone, make her comfortable, and let nature run its course.

"'She has signed a DNR, so when she stops breathing no efforts will be taken to prolong her life. She is a smart and strong-willed woman who knows her time is up.

"'Now is the time when you and anybody else that wants to, pay their last respects. I suspect she won't last another day or two at the most.'

"She patted me on the shoulder and praised me for being such a good daughter. As the tears ran down my cheek, I weakly whispered, 'I wish she was as good a mother.'

"The nurse's head jerked back, and she looked deeply into my eyes. She seemed to penetrate my mind, and after a few moments she empathetically uttered, 'Mother–daughter issues? There is a lot of that going around.'

"I called John, whom I have been in loose contact with, and explained the situation to him. While we had drifted apart, he still was a decent man with good values. He listened intently to my request for him to visit our dying mother.

"They hadn't seen each other in almost thirty years, and I knew there was bad blood between them. Neither would ever acknowledge the obvious, but Mom's face turned pale whenever it was brought up.

"He initially refused and came up with some lame excuses. I told him that whatever happened between he and Mom was in the past and she was still his mother. She brought him into this world and loved him dearly. I didn't mention my own feelings as I didn't want to appear selfish.

"'Rose, let's leave the past behind us. It's been too long and it's too late to make amends. She made her own bed and now she can sleep in it. I'm sorry to hear that she is dying, but she has led a long and comfortable life. My coming back won't change anything, and I just can't do it!'

"But I couldn't let him off the hook that easily. 'How do you think our dead father would feel if you weren't there? Mom is a broken, distraught old woman who lived through tough times. You haven't seen her for nearly thirty years.

"'Her life was indeed long, but far from easy! All her friends and relatives are gone. Our father died at a young age, and she never remarried. Her grown children, which just happens to be you and I, live far away and rarely visit her. She has lived through a century of depressions, wars, booming technology, and many hardships. She is a sick, lonely old woman who has lost her greatest love. That, by the way, just happens to be you! You can't let her leave this Earth without seeing you! You have always been and still are her favorite living person! I know something bad happened between you two, but let's forget that for now. This is the end – our last chance to make amends! Please, please come and say goodbye!'

"'Rose, you don't understand what she did to me. I just can't bring myself to see her. I am not an emotionally strong person; in fact, I am the opposite. I have made a life for myself here, and coming back would only bring an avalanche of bad memories. I live in the present and for the future. My past is nothing that I wish to revisit. Please understand.'

"I listened intently and did not interrupt him. I had always wondered what separated Mom and John. I was hoping to learn the truth.

"'John, I don't really care what the blowup between you two was about. The fact is our mother – *your* mother – is taking her last breaths. You were her favorite, and she still suffers from your separation. Just the sight of seeing you and showing that you care will ease her burden for eternity. You can't let her die without seeing you! Please, please, please, see her one last time!'

"There was silence at the other end of the line. I could hear my grown brother struggling to maintain his composure.

"I held my breath in anticipation of his answer. Had I done enough to convince him?

"In a shaky but deliberate voice he said, 'Okay, okay, I am on my way!'"

CHAPTER THIRTY-FIVE

"Mom was receiving home hospice care with an I.V. keeping her comfortable. I was sitting next to her in silence, concentrating on her shallow breaths and heart rate monitor.

"I was very nervous, as I knew John was on his way, but wondering if he would arrive too late. About noon, I heard a car pull up and a few seconds later heard footsteps from outdoors. I hurried to the window, but I just noticed a car pull away. No John. I returned to my chair downhearted, as I would have to face Mom's last breaths alone. Perhaps John changed his mind and decided not to come. As thoughts of being abandoned again dominated all else, the bedroom door slowly creaked open.

"My mother wasn't aware of the person walking in until my shriek startled her. I jumped up and hugged my brother, whom I hadn't seen in ten years. He looked haggard and tired from his red-eye flight.

"The years appeared to have treated him nicely. His hairline was receded with grey around the temples. He had forehead and crow's feet wrinkles, yet seemed at peace with his life. He hugged me as tears streamed down his cheeks.

"'Rose, it's good to see you after all these years. I am so sorry to have been away for so long. It was really selfish to abandon you and Mom like that. Please, please forgive me. I realize that running away didn't really solve anything; it just avoided the issue. Please just understand one thing: I had to get away!'

"My eyes caught his, and I locked his gaze. I let those last words sink in, fumed in silence, but decided to let it go.

"'I'm so glad you're here. You have no idea what this means to Mom and me. The doctors say that the end is imminent. I have been hoping that you would make it in time, and luckily you have. Seeing you will make her last hours peaceful.

"'One of these days you really should explain yourself; after all, we are brother and sister. If there is anybody that should have left, it was me. You were always the favorite, and I was always the black sheep! But we will save that for another time, big brother.'

"I gave him another big hug which he reciprocated. Grabbing his hand, I brought him over to Mom's bed and aroused her.

"Initially she didn't respond, and I thought that she may have lapsed into a coma. Slowly, and at first muttering some incohesive words, her eyes opened. She searched the room with glassy eyes until she spotted John.

"She let out a gasp and her pupils visibly dilated. Tears flowed weakly down her cheeks and an apprehensive look appeared on her face. She seemed to be asking herself if it was really her long estranged son.

"John walked by me and planted a light kiss on Mom's forehead. 'Yeah, it's me, Mom, your poor excuse for a son, John. I'm sorry I have stayed away for so long; there is no excuse for my behavior!'

"Even though she would die in a few hours, she still had all her marbles. In a weak but firm voice she said, 'You are wrong,

John; you had a great reason to stay away. I'm sure the sight of me and what I did to you was too much to bear. Believe me, there is not a day that goes by that I don't regret my actions. If I could do anything to change the past, I surely would. As much as I've missed you, I'm glad you broke free and started a new life.

"'Rose told me you joined an artist colony, married a nice girl, and seem content. Even though I have missed you, I'm ecstatic that you overcame my mistakes and have made a life for yourself.

"'I can't repair the damage and will die with unforgivable guilt, but you being here has lifted my spirits. I don't care if you don't forgive me. I'm just grateful that you have led a decent life. Thank you for being here; I am ready to die in peace now!'

Rose paused her story and looked Cynthia straight into her eyes. "I was in a state of bewilderment. What the hell were they talking about? Mom apologizing to John for what she did to him? What the hell was going on? Mom gave John everything! She gave me nothing!"

Rose continued her story. "'Okay, okay people,' I found myself raising my voice. 'I know this is not the best time or place, but what the hell are you two talking about?

"'I have lived a shitty, screwed up life in part due to low self-esteem since childhood. I am a mental case saddled with depression, relationship issues, and dependence on psychiatric drugs. My shrink says its origin is probably from parents or a *parent* who paid little attention to me. Mom, we all know that you clearly favored John and basically ignored me. Don't try to deny the truth; I have seen your frowns when I needed or interacted with you.'

"As Mom tried to interrupt, I wagged my finger at her. 'Let me continue; I deserve to speak my piece!

"Now, let me get this straight. John got all the attention, John got all the help, John got all the better everything. Little Rose gets shit. John runs away because of something you did to him! I can't fathom what the hell you two are talking about! Will somebody please enlighten me?!'

"After taking in my unexpected outburst, John and Mom remained quiet. They lowered their eyes, and John shuffled his feet as Mom looked at her blanket. I folded my arms over my chest and started tapping my foot. The room became uncomfortably still as nobody was budging.

"I waited a few minutes and John tried to excuse himself by saying he needed to use the bathroom. I blocked his way and said, 'Over my dead body! Nobody is leaving this room to pee or die until I find out what the hell is going on.'

"Both John and Mom looked at each other as if asking if they should confess the truth. John put up his hands in surrender, and Mom came to a decision.

"'Rose, dear,' she weakly asked, 'what gives you the idea that I don't love you? Where did you come up with that?'

"'Mom, don't play games with me. When I was only seven, I heard you tell Dad you hated me because I looked just like your own mother. It was at night when you both thought I was asleep.'

"As white as she was, my mother's skin tone got even paler. She started to say something, but I cut her off.

"'Don't deny that you said it; it is buried in my soul and I am not mistaken. You said it. And worse than that, you were my caretaker rather than my mother my entire life.

"My mom stopped trying to talk as she recalled that night. She buried her face in her boney, arthritic hands. Taking a few seconds to compose herself she said, 'Rose, I had no idea that you heard that marital fight so many years ago. No, I won't deny that I said it. But this is the truth so help me God. It was a lie. Your father was berating me for not paying much attention to you. He threatened to leave me and take you with him unless I changed my behavior. While it is true that you resembled my mother whom I didn't really like, I still loved you. Still, I admit that I favored John at your expense. I never realized how much it affected you! It seems that I have screwed up two children. I love you just as much as John, but I just couldn't spread my love equally.

"'As much as I screwed you up, I did a far worse thing to John. I tried to make up for my sins *too* much. I'm so, so sorry, Rose. Please forgive me!'

"I stood, bewildered and disbelieving. A few words after a lifetime of suffering and feeling unwanted didn't cut it for me. I knew Mom was hours from death but I couldn't contain my boiling anger!

"'You lied to Dad that you disliked me, but yet ignored me all these years. Sorry, that makes no sense at all. What kind of person are you? Now you want me to forgive you? I should have left for California instead of John.'

"Mom lowered her head and didn't respond. I started to storm out the door at this unexpected blast from the past. I thought to myself, *Bullshit. That is the worst thought out lie I have ever heard. She loved me as much as John? Nonsense!* I didn't believe her for two seconds. My life in shambles, fifty years of neglect, lying about something she said decades ago. *What kind of fool does she think I am?*

"As I made for the door, anger seething through every cell of my body, John suddenly blocked my path. 'Rose, please sit down. Mom and I both have something to tell you.'

ONE HUNDRED YEARS WITHOUT LOVE

"Anger controlled all my other senses and reflexively I attempted to push him aside. With surprising strength, he lifted me off the floor and plopped me down on a chair. 'You will listen to what Mom will tell you!'

"Looking directly at the dying old woman, he said, 'Mom, it is time to come clean. She deserves to know the truth. She has earned it, and maybe it will free her from some of her demons. In hindsight, we should have told her years ago.'

"Slow to respond, Mom nodded her head. 'Yeah, John, I guess you are right. But telling the truth about the ultimate sin is not easy for an old woman.'

"My mind was in chaos. The ultimate sin? What the hell did she do to him?

"Mom hesitated, took several deep breaths, and bravely said, 'Okay, Rose, here goes. I can't believe after all these years, I'm finally spilling my guts. Rose, you have no idea the guilt and stress I have been living with since John was born.'

"Turning towards John, she choked out, 'You know something, John? I was dreading the day when I might have to admit my sins. After all, it did drive you away!

"'I already feel a weight lifting of my chest. Keeping it inside did me little good. For that matter, if Rose knew the truth back then she may have understood me better. I never even considered the effects it may have caused my other child. I should have confided in Rose a long time ago.'

"Swiveling back towards me she pleaded, 'Please try to forgive. I'm not proud of what I did, and I do regret it every waking moment. I truly never realized how much it affected *you*. I guess I am not so observant to other people's feelings.'"

Cynthia, in suspense, was holding Molly so tightly that the little Pomeranian yelped in discomfort. "Oops. I'm sorry, Molly."

She returned her gaze back to the seemingly transformed Rose and said, "Before you continue, I just can't believe how good you look. Your face is so rosy, your hair is shimmering, and you seem energized.' Is it my imagination, or did something amazing happen to you?"

"No, you are not crazy. Something magical did happen. It seems like my mom, the cold-hearted Esther Shapiro, never really despised me. She loved, and still loves, me as much as John. It's just that there were circumstances that made her act as she did."

Cynthia felt a warm flush coursing through her heart as she realized Rose's lifelong burden was lifted. In hopeful disbelief, she had to hear it again. "What, what did you just say?"

CHAPTER THIRTY-SIX

"Yeah, it's true! Mom really did love me; it's just that John needed more attention. It seems that Mom was a heavy smoker during her pregnancy with John. She got addicted at a young age, like most young people in those days. Cigarettes were cheap, and the dangers weren't known at the time. It was widely accepted to smoke; as a matter of fact, all the cool kids did it.

"By the 1950s, doctors were becoming aware of the dangers, but the government didn't issue warnings until the early sixties. My father was never a smoker and despised Mom's habit. He used to remind her of how she reeked of the smell and what a waste of money they were.

"Being an avid newspaper reader, he was learning that doctors were noticing serious illnesses to smokers and their unborn children. She made a halfhearted effort to quit but couldn't. She also hid this little tidbit from my father as they both suspected that cigarette smoking was indeed dangerous.

"Mom went into labor two months early with John, and he was born at only four and a half pounds. His lungs were weak, and he was put in an incubator with oxygen pumped in. It was touch and go for a while, but he obviously made it.

"Mom lied like the dickens when the doctors asked her if she had smoked while pregnant. They looked doubtfully as she denied the accusations.

"The guilt was too much for her to admit, and she feared my father would divorce her.

"Their marriage was already somewhat shaky, mostly due to Mom's uncontrollable temper. She often went into tantrums and anger fits for the smallest slight or incident. Dad always told her to calm down and not to flip out over such little things.

"He informed her that neighbors were calling her a crazy lady, and not only was it embarrassing but the stress was becoming unbearable. He often claimed that he loved her, but didn't know if he could continue living with her.

"Even though John survived, he suffered some respiratory and brain damage. He was slow to develop and was always a poor student. His IQ was in the low normal range, and he suffered from childhood asthma.

"Mom kept the truth from everybody, but she suffered in silence. She told us there wasn't a day that she didn't feel the guilt of being a contemptible mother.

"She gave John all the love, attention, money, and resources that she could. She kept him right next to her in the bed, which further infuriated my dad.

"Any little sniffle or cough sent my mom into a panic. The doctor made many a house call during John's younger years. When I came along, it was purely by accident and Mom didn't have room for any distractions or additional people needing her attention.

"My father and myself were too much baggage for her to handle and we became second fiddle. Dad compensated by being away a lot and having extra-marital affairs. Mom became aware of his infidelities but looked the other way. Her guilt did not allow her to be outraged.

"I, on the other hand, had nothing to fall back on."

CHAPTER THIRTY-SEVEN

"But, Mom, just because John had problems doesn't mean it was from the smoking. Didn't most people from your generation smoke?"

"Besides, the dangers at that time weren't even realized. I've seen old movies where doctors were smoking while examining patients, teachers smoking during class, and ashtrays being used in everybody's homes."

"His issues could easily have been coincidental. Plenty of premature babies had non-smoking mothers, and plenty of people have learning disabilities. Don't be so hard on yourself; just because John wasn't a good student, doesn't mean anything. Not everybody gets straight A's. John, like all of us, has strengths and weaknesses."

I looked at my brother and spoke highly of his best qualities. "He is a phenomenal artist and always has been. He has the heart of a lion, and I'm sure he is a loving husband."

John smiled.

Mom replied, "Maybe it was the smoking, maybe not. I still didn't do the right thing by my child. His whole life may have turned out differently if I behaved better! I was mentally too weak to break the habit. I was selfish not to try harder or seek some help. In any scenario, I did, in fact, know that it could potentially harm my baby."

"'Rose, I never told what I'm about to tell you to anybody except John. Do you remember when he dropped out in his first year of college?'

Rose nodded and mumbled, "Mom, not everybody can hack college. It is extremely rough, and John always struggled in school. It wasn't a great shock to me that he dropped out."

Mom continued, "He became so distraught that he went into a depression. While his friends were in class, he was sitting home watching game shows and sitcoms. He started drinking and smoking marijuana. He stayed in the basement and slept most of the day.

I myself felt shame and guilt for his problems and became desperate. I tried my best to lift his spirits, suggested other careers, and offered to pay for tutors, but he was too distraught. He insisted he was just a fuckup and had convinced himself that he'd never amount to anything.

He told me he was a worthless failure!"

Mom cried as she recounted the scene from so many years before. "I tried to hug him, but he just pushed me aside, telling me that he was aware of all the special treatment I gave him. He realized my poor treatment of you, Rose, and your father, even before I had fully acknowledged it myself."

Mom looked at him and covered her face in shame. "I never realized it was so obvious. In my mind I was doing the right thing and protecting the person I'd damaged the most."

John stopped her there and said, "I probably should have told you to love everybody equally, but I did love the attention. While I was different from everybody else, I felt special being around you!"

John remembered the scene with his mother from some many years ago. He relayed the life altering events that enfolded.

"Now that must all change. I give up on this world. In spite of all you have given, I am still a screw-up. There is nothing else you can do."

"'No, no, John. You are not a screw up; I am the screw up!'

I looked directly into her eyes and sincerely said, "Oh, Mom, it's not your fault; some kids just aren't right. The parents aren't to blame; once you give birth it's our life. We succeed or screw up all on our own. I know you devoted your life to me, but ultimately it comes down to me being an oddball."

Mom blurted out her confession. "'There is not a day that goes by that I don't wish I could alter the past! I have kept this secret inside for so long, but my day of reckoning can't be avoided.'

With her head lowered, Mom sobbed and said "I smoked like a chimney when I was pregnant with you. You were an innocent living creature, totally dependent on me for proper neonatal care and I screwed up. You undoubtedly received less oxygen to your brain. I knew the dangers, and yet I was too weak and selfish to give it up!"

"'We can make all the excuses in the world, but it was me. I knew the dangers and hid my smoking from your father and the doctors. It was me; I caused all your problems!'

It took a few seconds for me to process this confession. All the years of pent-up frustration and failure after failure seemed to come together. I can distinctly recall my immediate reaction. *'Is this why I can't seem to do anything right?'*

Mom continued. "When I saw you in the incubator, barely alive, much less thriving, I realized the damage I had caused you. The warnings the medical profession were giving and the smoking industry denying were the truth! My weakness and denial of the warnings are the cause of your problems!"

Mom buried her face and repeated over and over, "It was me, it was me! I tried my best to help you! I put a hundred and fifty percent into you.

Looking back on things, I now realize I neglected your sister and my marriage. It was an unconscious act of redemption."

She lifted her head and looked intently into my eyes. "'Please, please don't give up! We will find an outlet for your unique talents. Everybody has his or her strong and weak qualities. Academics are not your specialty, but you are a great drawer and artist. Perhaps you can focus on that."

"I sat in the chair beneath the window and a wave of emotional memories like a tsunami came over me. "I was always the dumbest kid in class. The other kids constantly belittled me. They would call me retard, dumb, and stupid. I remember the look of frustration from my special ed. teachers who scolded me for not concentrating enough.

Yet they were wrong. I put all my energy and soul into trying to do better. Despite all my efforts, things just didn't stick or click into place. The academic world didn't make sense to me. Two times two equals what? How did the other kids know the correct answer? While the other kids were using paper and pencil to do the math, I got so frustrated that I drew faces on the numbers and letters and gave them human characteristics. The zeroes, O's, D's, G's, and Q's were fat people. The ones, I's, L's, and T's were skinny people. The F's had long noses and so on.

One teacher walked by and asked what I was doing; reminding me that there was no place for art in math class. I told her I couldn't do the math. She told me I was lucky I could draw because my math skills were horrible!

That intended insult enlightened me; she said I was good at something!

ONE HUNDRED YEARS WITHOUT LOVE

Why did the other kids catch the ball while I got clunked on the head? Sports and gym were just as frustrating as academics. I was also prone to sudden and uncontrollable emotional outbursts. When asked why I would suddenly start crying, I couldn't ever provide an answer. After a while, my self-esteem hit rock bottom and I was a clinically depressed child, which carried over to my teenage years.

Fortunately, my high school grew weary of me and allowed me to graduate, despite all my academic failures. A two-year vocational college accepted me and there was a reason for hope. A new beginning awaited. That summer between high school graduation and the first year of college provided a beacon of light for my future.

I would look up from bed before falling asleep and think to myself, nobody at this college knows me. I will work extra hard and take easy classes. Screw the math, the grammar, and the chemistry. I'll buy some new clothes; I will be outgoing and make new friends. Perhaps some girl will notice me, and we can hit it off. The future seemed better than the past.

Alas, college was no better than high school. While nobody made fun of me, academics were impossible, even the easy classes. I was required to take introduction classes in English and Math, despite wanting to be an Art major, which was overwhelming.

I did however join the art club and flourished there. The club leader, Mrs. Merrill, was very impressed with my work. One day she told me I was a very talented artist and invited me to be the co-leader of the art club.

I'd always thought my drawings were good, but I'd never had a teacher or adult, besides my mother, give me special recognition. The rest of the semester I loved art club and made friends with club members. We would hang out on weekends, and I developed some good friendships. I grew particularly interested in a skinny, fair skinned, shy freshman in the club. She reciprocated my advances.

But it all came crashing down when I failed three midterms. I was put on academic probation and eventually kicked out of school.

I tried so hard in school to bring home grades like Rose. I always sensed that my brain couldn't function like others. Was I destined to be stupid, or did Mom's smoking cause me brain damage? Was I a dumbass because of her?

As much as I hated to admit it, I had to conclude that it was true. Mom caused my problems and ruined my entire life!"

"'Mom, I have to go!' I pushed her hand away as she asked for forgiveness.

"'I need to time to process what you just told me. While I'm sure you didn't mean to harm me, you most likely did. Smoking during pregnancy is *now* well known to reduce oxygen to a developing baby's brain. You will always be my mother, and I will always love you, but for now I need to get away from you!"

"As I paced around the room, I shouted out loud to nobody and everybody, 'Oh, my God, I am brain damaged! It all makes sense now! Lack of oxygen from my mom's smoking left me an idiot!'"

"As Mom pleaded for me to talk to her, I abruptly ended the conversation. *'Mom, don't say another word! You have done enough already! Please, leave me alone!'*

"And that's why I left for California and never returned!"

CHAPTER THIRTY-EIGHT

An enraptured Cynthia was a whirlwind of emotions. *Oh, my God, she thought. Esther and Rose's entire lives were affected by circumstances beyond their control.*

Esther's entire being was shaped by the Great Depression and being unloved by an overburdened, coldish mother in distress.

Rose's fate was sealed when that unloved child, Esther, smoked like a chimney during her own pregnancy and damaged her oldest child. Damn the tobacco industry! Rose suffered the mental consequences more than the actual victim. The devil works in mysterious ways.

"But, Rose," she said, "Why do you seem so cheerful? Your mother just died, and you found out that your brother suffered fetal damage from maternal smoking."

With a look of serenity, and in a nonchalant tone, Rose continued. "Of course I'm upset that Mom is dead, but the fact of the matter is that we are all destined to die.

"Mom lived longer than most, and she was a lonely, sick woman. Almost all her family, friends, and neighbors were no longer around. Besides all those earthly changes, she carried terrible emotional burdens all of her life.

"She was an unintended birth during the Great Depression. Her own mother viewed her as an extra mouth to feed and a burden. She grew up feeling unloved by everybody but her father.

"Then when she married, she couldn't give up smoking and inadvertently damaged her firstborn child. After barely surviving birth, she watched him struggle day in and day out. He came home depressed and failed at most things. I'm sure she suffered twice as much knowing she caused his problems.

"At the end, she died with both her son and daughter by her side forgiving her. I am confident that she is in a better place and her soul is at rest! While I am not a religious person, I suspect she is at peace and reunited with her loved ones."

Cynthia sat quietly and let Rose continue.

"As for my brother, he is a happy man! He overcame his handicaps and made a life for himself. Sure, he undoubtedly had a rough beginning and suffered immensely. God only knows the inner torment he suffered. Yet, he overcame his handicaps and broke free only because Mom finally mustered the courage to tell him the truth. Sure, it would have been better if none of this happened in the first place. Unfortunately, we don't get a dress rehearsal for life.

"By escaping to California, he started fresh and concentrated on what he was good at. Secretly he told me he felt relieved that his problems were not because of anything he did. He is content!

"As for me, it seems that even though Mom treated me poorly and may have even disliked my presence, it was not because of anything I did. I'm sure my similar appearance to my grandmother gave her an extra unconscious reason to ignore me. In truth, it was a somewhat expected reaction to give John most of the love.

"In fact, her greatest act of love may have been quitting smoking during her pregnancy with me. While that doesn't erase sixty years of neglect and a tough life, I know I am not to blame. I now know my low self-esteem, mood swings, and inability to form good relationships were normal for an unloved child. Yet it seems that mom actually did love me the only way possible for her under the circumstances.

"I feel much better about myself. The dark cloud hanging over my whole life has suddenly allowed the sun to shine. I understand it all now!"

She looked up and to no one in particular repeated the phrase, "I understand it now. I understand it now. It was not me!"

Cynthia just shook her head. "Rose, you are a better person than me. After all you went through, to have that sense of understanding is remarkable. I don't think I could be as forgiving as you!"

"Well, dear, that is what thirty years of psychotherapy will do for a person. I have learned to be very introspective and have learned that people behave as they do for a reason. That reason is usually due to their past and not the present!

"I do forgive my mother, but I can never erase or forget my past. I am forever affected and molded into the person I am because of her. Whatever time I have left, I will never blame myself for my shortcomings!"

"So, you are okay with your mom's passing?"

"Actually, I am both relieved that her earthly unhappiness is gone, and it seems that she also made amends with her own mother."

Cynthia's face blanched for a few seconds, trying to digest that last sentence. "What did you just say?"

"Yeah, I said what you heard. It seems that she made up with her own deceased mother, Jenny Shapiro."

Rose put up her hands. "Do you want to hear the weirdest thing? You may not believe this, but *minutes* before mom passed, she closed her eyes and started talking."

Cynthia, not knowing what to say, just listened in stunned silence.

Rose continued. "We could tell the end was very near as her pulse rate was slowing down and her speech was becoming incoherent. She started to lapse into unconsciousness with sudden abrupt incoherent awakenings. John and I became silent and each one of us held one of her bony hands.

"I was just a torrent of emotions. I was saddened that my mother was passing but at the same time I was still belligerent at how she had treated me. Even though on her deathbed I discovered the reasons for her actions, it still didn't erase my miserable past. Apologizing and saying she secretly loved me doesn't erase the scars. Oh, how all ours loves would have been different if she heeded the warnings of smoking during pregnancy!

"Anyway, enough about me. John and I were startled as Mom suddenly opened her eyes wide and stared at the heavens.

"In a strong voice she said, "Miriam, what are you doing here? Why are you floating above my bed?' There was silence for a few moments. 'No, no, I can't go with you; John and Rose are here now. Maybe in a few minutes.'

"John and I were stunned to say the least. Miriam was our cousin, Aunt Judy's daughter, and was also on her deathbed in upstate New York. We didn't say a word and assumed it was delirium before death. We subsequently found out that Miriam had died about ten minutes before Mom passed away!

"Still staring up at the heavens, Mom continued. 'Mom, Mom? Is that you?' There was no confusion; she thought she was talking to her own dead mother, my grandmother, Jenny Shapiro. 'What did you say? You're coming to bring me home? But I want Dad to bring me back. You never really wanted me when you were alive and now you want me? Where is my father?'

"John and I were mesmerized by Mom's spiel. There were a few moments of silence again and we heard her pulse rate monitor slow down. Her breathing became weaker, and the color was draining from her face. We could sense the end was imminent!

"'You are sorry for the way you treated me? What are you saying?

Dad will meet me, and Sissy and Judy are waiting also? You all have been anxiously waiting for me? But why you, of all people, to take me? You have hated me my entire life.'

"Her pulse increased ever so slightly as she got very agitated.

"In a weakening voice she said, 'Oh, now you are sorry for not loving me. My whole childhood you neglected me, and I felt like a piece of extra baggage. Please send Papa to get me; he was the only one that truly loved me!'

"There was a long pause as Mom closed her eyes. John and I were stone silent, taking in this spectacle. We both weren't sure if Mom was delusional or if an extra spiritual event was taking place.

"'I know times were tough and you were overburdened by working two jobs and running the household. Yeah, I know you were born privileged and expected not to be burdened so.' Another pause, and then, 'Oh, horseshit; you married dad because you fell in love, and life didn't work out as you expected. I was probably an accident, and the Great Depression hit. I was still your daughter and deserved better!'

"More silence and Mom's pulse rate dropped dramatically. Her pupils dilated and tears ran from her eyes. She stopped blinking as her heart monitor started to flatten out.

"'Okay, Mom I understand. Love was sparse in those tough times and since you have departed you have watched over me. As the burden of love was too much to give during your time on Earth, you have loved me with all you heart since then!'

"'Yes, I do believe you, and I am getting a warm feeling inside of me. I feel my spiritual energy surging and a feeling of love and bliss surrounding me, even as my physical body is almost lifeless. Yes, yes, yes! I will go with you!'

"Mom, with all her remaining strength, weakly raised her arms as if waiting for an embrace. 'I await your love and am ready to reunite with all. I forgive you!'

"With that last word, Mom's arms dropped, her eyes closed, and she took her last breath. John and I felt a rush of warm air rise from her deathbed up to the heavens. It may have been my imagination or the tension of the moment, but I thought I heard two women above us whisper to each other, 'I love you!'